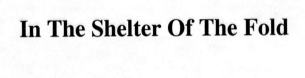

In The Shelter Of The Fold

Other Published works by Kenneth Robbins:

Novels:
Buttermilk Bottoms, Winner of the Toni Morrison Prize for Fiction and the Associated Writing Programs Novel Award.

The Baptism of Howie Cobb

Plays:
Molly's Rock
The Hunger Feast
The Dallas File
The War Woman of Wauhatchee Creek

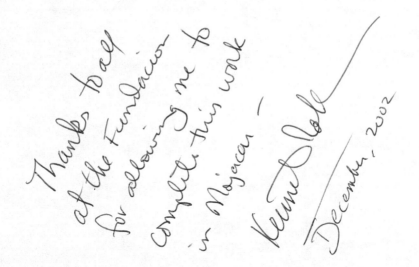

Thanks to all
at the Fundacion
for allowing me to
complete this work
in Mojacar —

Kenneth Robbins

December, 2002

In The Shelter Of The Fold

Kenneth Robbins

Dream Catcher Publishing, Inc.

In The Shelter of The Fold

A Novel

By Kenneth Robbins

Published by

Dream Catcher Publishing, Inc.
P.O. Box 95783
Atlanta, Georgia 30347
Fax: 888-771-2800
Email: DCP@DreamCatcherPublishing.net

ISBN 0-9720495-5-X

Library of Congress Control Number 2002114077

Printed: Printed Prince Media Group, USA 404 851.1763

Acknowledgements:

"I offer sincere thanks to the Japan Foundation, Tokyo, Japan, for providing me with the opportunity through a Japan Foundation Artists Fellowship to research and write a major portion of *IN THE SHELTER OF THE FOLD*. I am thankful to the Fundacion Valparaiso in Mojacar, Spain, for the chance to complete the novel while in residence the summer of 2001. I especially thank Dwan Hightower of Dream Catcher Publishing for her faith in my work. And finally, I thank my wife, Dorothy Dodge Robbins, Ph.D., for her support of my writing habit as well as her remarkable insights as editor, and friend."

For my Brother, James Aubrey Robbins, Jr.
(1942- 2001)

The Ninety and Nine

There were ninety and nine that safely lay
In the shelter of the fold,
But one was out on the hills away,
Far-off from the gates of gold.
   Away on the mountains wild and bare,
   Away from the tender shepherd's care;
   Away from the tender shepherd's care.

"Lord, Thou has here Thy ninety and nine;
Are they not enough for Thee?"
But the Shepherd made answer: "This of Mine
Has wandered away from me;
   And although the road be rough and steep,
   I go to the desert to find my sheep;
   I go to the desert to find my sheep."

But none of the ransomed ever knew
How deep were the waters crossed;
Nor how dark was the night that the Lord passed thro'

   Ere He found His sheep that was lost.
   Out in the desert He heard its cry--
   Sick and helpless, and ready to die.
   Sick and helpless, and ready to die.

--Elizabeth C. Clephane

CHAPTER ONE
Indella Shealy Cobb Gives Birth To Her Second Son

1

Indella Shealy Cobb took a look at her newborn baby and said: "Take it away it's not mine I don't want it take it away please!"

Nobody but Glory Bea blamed her. The baby weighed twelve pounds eleven ounces, a difficult birth, eighteen hours, and he was bald and he was a he. She already had a male child. What did she need another one for?

"What's come over you, daughter," demanded Glory Bea, newly made a grandmother for the second time. "Ain't you got more sense than that? The child's yourn and you're to take it, love it, and help it grow."

But the new mother would not be consoled. She was only a baby herself, just turned eighteen by two days and already the caretaker of a husky male child called Howbo who was still in diapers and demanded more of her time and her yanked-on breasts than she ever dreamed possible. So what need did she have for another boy child, just like the first, with a bald head and a penis and not the girl she longed for, the baby girl she was to call Sandra Ellen and dress in pink dresses and show off throughout the Village. But this "thing?" this lump of screaming flesh, what need did she have for it?

"Take it away, I don't want it, it's not mine, so take it away!" she yelled louder than before, hoping somebody, maybe that hag of a wet nurse, Mabel Lane, would hear and do what she bid. Instead, Mabel Lane spat her snuff-ridden saliva into a dirty pinto bean can, and Glory Bea clung to the child, now washed clean of birthing fluids and wrapped in a coarse army blanket, held it close, the poor little unwanted thing. She would love it if her daughter couldn't. She'd care for it and help it grow to a man. And she said, "Shame on you, Indella, acting this way. What's Dr. Hamilton going to think!"

"Let him think what he wants, it's not mine, somebody made a mistake. I want my baby girl." And she cried herself to sleep, not once touching the newborn boy or offering its hungry mouth the faucet to her overflowing breast.

2

Howbo hated the newcomer. All it did was yell and sapped away everybody's attention. It refused Glory Bea's sugar-teats; spat out warm milk spooned into its mouth, and gnawed the wet nurse's nipple, almost drawing blood.

"Ain't having nothing else to do with that blasted child," the wet nurse declared and walked out of the house, head high, not to return. "That nasty Indella Cobb can suckle her own young and good riddance," was her parting shot.

Howbo was crawling those days and he could find himself in all kinds of places where he did not belong. Like on top of the sink. Glory Bea discovered him there, rummaging among the unwashed dishes. "Heaven's sake," she announced. "Ain't you the rascal. How'd you get yourself this far off the floor, Little Mister?"

Howbo did not know any words, otherwise he would have answered. Instead he glared at the crib that held the bawling intruder and wished he had been successful in locating the carving knife he knew was kept somewhere on top of the sink.

"Rambunctious Howbo" was what Momma Cobb called him. Papa Cobb called him something different, and

Glory Bea did not like her grandchildren around anybody who would nickname one of them "Rasputin." She was unsure exactly who Rasputin was, but the name called up images she did not care for in the least. Images of hell and damnation and brimstone. So her nicknames for Howbo were safe: Little Mister and sometimes Buster Brown. Both fit, too, from her point of view.

As far as Howbo was concerned, there was nothing good about the newcomer. He smelled of puke and dirty diapers. He had no sense of time or place, crying day and night, giving nobody any peace. And he took attention, attention that rightfully belonged to the first born.

Howbo crawled to the little homemade crib where the baby cried. Maybe he could get the stupid idiot to shut up. He took a firm grip on one of the spindles and tugged on it rocking the crib back and forth. Even with the rocking, the baby still screamed, increasing rather than decreasing its volume. So he tugged harder. It was not working, his efforts to get the lump of screaming flesh to hush. He tugged still harder until, finally, the crib with baby and all, toppled over, dumping the infant onto the floor with a thud.

The baby screamed even louder, only different this time. Instead of a call for food, the infant yelped in terror, bringing Glory Bea with all her adult love-giving scurrying to the rescue. That did not please Howbo. That was not want he had intended at all. What he wanted was a little quiet, the way things had been before the newcomer showed up.

Judging from the reaction to the toppled baby, flipping the crib was not the thing to do. He determined he would refrain from doing such a thing again.

Glory Bea turned her scalding eyes on Little Mister. "What has gotten into you, Buster Brown? What in Heaven's name possesses you to do such wicked things?"

Howbo did not have the words to tell her. If he could have formed the words, they would have been: "I want my life back the way it was."

3

"You've got to give the little one a name, Indella," Glory Bea scolded her daughter. "It's been almost a week and that poor Dr. Hamilton's not had a chance to fill in the birth certificate yet."

"Sandra Ellen," the teenaged mother said.

"You know you can't name a male child such a thing as that."

"I don't want a male child," she said and turned away. Indella was still in her birthing clothes, still not ready to return to the world of being mother as well as daughter, wife, caretaker of a house, and proprietor of her own soul. She did not care to "come around," as her mother called it, "and make something of all this." What she wanted was a daughter of her own, a baby she could play house with, dress up in pretty pink dresses and take out in the tram and show the world how beautiful a daughter she and her recently drafted husband, Howell Madison Cobb, could produce. Nothing else interested her, not even Howbo with his pleas for attention. As far as the newcomer was concerned, they could take it to the city dump. She wanted nothing to do with it.

"How long you plan on pouting, Miss Pris?" her mother asked.

"Not pouting."

"Seems like it to me. And what do you think that husband of yourn is gonna say when he comes home and he has a no-name baby to deal with?"

"Let him think what he wants. If he was interested, he'd be here now, wouldn't he?"

"You know he can't be here. He's off up there in Virginia, getting ready to fight for his country."

"I need him home, Momma," Indella wailed, new streams of tears flowing down her pudgy, pampered cheeks. Her crying started Howbo again. It was like a duet of woe, a competition to see who could make the most noise. With such a racket, the newcomer finally hushed, the first time in a week, only with both Indella and Howbo in tip-top voice, nobody noticed.

4

On the seventh day, Dr. Hamilton came to Glory Bea's whitewashed house on the outskirts of town. He had not been back since the baby's first deep-throated cry. Now he stood on the threshold of the Shealy house and held out the unsigned birth certificate, hoping somebody in the house would finally do their Christian duty.

"Got to sign it," he said, "else I'm breaking the law."

"What law," Indella asked.

"Law what says I've got to complete a birthing certificate before I leave the site of the birth. It's been a week, ma'am, and the law may be lenient with some but not that lenient. Sheriff came by this morning and says to me, get that baby named today or else."

"Else what?"

"Damned if I want to find out. Excuse the French, Glory Bea. But this daughter of yours is downright bullheaded."

"Always been that way, Doc Ham. Ever since you helped me bring her into this world."

"Sorry to say she's making me regret my participation in that event, Glory Bea."

"Just leave the paper with me, sir," Glory Bea said under her breath, "and I'll bring it down to your office signed and sealed. That's a promise."

He left, shaking his head. He had been part of almost a hundred and fifty birthings in all his days but this was his first major rejection, a mother not wanting the product of her womb. The world was changing and he did not care for the direction it was going.

Glory Bea sat at her kitchen table with pen in hand. Things were finally quiet for a few minutes as all three of her babies, Indella, Howbo, and the unnamed infant, decided to take naps. She turned on her RCA radio. She could only get one station, the one from Atlanta, and it was fuzzy most of the time. For some reason today it was clear and the voice she heard was that of that British fellow. The one in charge of their war effort against the hated Hitler, announcing something or other to do with the American forces under some general she had never heard of, a general with a name that sounded German to her. She did not pay much attention as she put the pen to work on the empty birth certificate.

That afternoon, when Glory Bea returned the signed certificate to his office on Pine Crest Avenue, Doctor Hamilton knew it was forged, that Indella had not put her name to the piece of paper, though it was there for him to read. But that mattered little. The paper was signed, the child had a name, and all was again well.

He glanced to the appropriate space and read: "Winston Churchill Cobb." Now what woman in her right mind would want to lumber a stalwart, energetic young American boy with such a highfalutin British name! He smirked. Just wait until the kid gets to school and has to face down the bullies with a name like that. Winston Churchill Cobb. Regardless, it was better than no name at all.

5

On the eighth day, Indella gave the newborn, little Winnie-Pooh as Glory Bea called him, her breast. Not because she wanted to but, because it hurt more than she needed if she continued to refuse. Howbo on one breast, little Winnie-Pooh on the other. Tug of war.

"This ain't the way it's supposed to be," the teenaged mother complained. "Momma," she said to Glory Bea, "you had you a little baby girl. Why can't I?"

"Patience, child," was Glory Bea's response. "Time's on your side."

"Time be--," but Indella could not say it. If she used the big "D" word, she would burn an eternity in hell. Besides, Glory Bea would wash her mouth out with laundry detergent regardless of her age and her new fangled adulthood. But time was not her friend, not the way Glory Bea had it all planned. Time was the thing she did not feel she had much of. She was old, almost twenty, and besides, as her Momma implied, there would be time for more birthings. No sir, not her. Having children was too much work. No more and never again. Howbo had been enough to last her a lifetime. It was her longing for a baby girl that had prompted her to give motherhood a second round. With Howbo, labor had been nearly twenty hours and then he had come out just fine in spite of all the pulling and tugging and pushing. And now Winnie-Pooh was eighteen hours of even more excruciating pain, and see what it had gained her. All that work for the ugliest little baby boy she had ever seen.

Her compelling question was what to do with that fancy-style pink jumper that cost her half a week's pay at the Franklin Five and Dime? Give it away? Use it for dusting? Frame it and hang it on the wall above her bed? Or keep it? For what, another try? Heaven forbid. If

Howell Madison Cobb wanted another child, he could deliver it himself. Indella had no intention of going through the process a third time. Besides, she had another idea. Indella had it all planned in her head for when Howie came home on leave. She would have Howbo dressed in his little sailor suit and Sandra Ellen prissing around in her pretty pink jumper. Then she and her husband whom she loved more than life itself would parade through town, her clutching his arm and him beaming with pride over what they had done together. The picture in her head was camera-ready.

So it's only natural, inevitable more than likely, that on the first day Glory Bea left her daughter home alone with her two babies, Indella put Winnie-Pooh, a child she kept calling Sandra, in the pretty little pink jumper. It looked right, almost like it was meant to be. The baby's healthy tummy fit perfectly inside the pink lace. And if you looked at him close enough, you could see his fat pink cheeks and the shine in his eyes and the cute way he had of sucking on his fat little thumb. Plus, he was growing hair on his head, fine, curly red hair that wanted to curl its way into his ears. It was not long before there was enough hair to sport not one but two pretty little pink bows. And didn't he look lovely? Just like the little girl she so desperately wanted and felt she had earned. After all, a baby's a baby, right? There's no such thing as sex for children under the age of ten. One child is the same as the other and that is the way God meant it to be. So what does it matter? Little Sandra Ellen looked perfectly charming wearing pink. Won't Howie be pleased when he comes home?

"Momma Cobb," she said with pride, "I'm gonna come visit yawl one of these days. Me and my babies."

And Momma Cobb said she could wait thank you very much.

6

Momma Cobb was not blessed with the quality others called patience. She had too many children of her own, eight if you counted them, to find patience worth waiting on. First her oldest, big and handsome Heviathan with his huge laugh and eager handshake had married Marlys Abbrams and that was good. Marlys had been born to be a mother and a wife and Momma Cobb was pleased that her eldest son, the one who was intended to be her helpmate as she and Alexander Stevens Cobb entered their declining years, had made such a wise choice in a bride. Hev and Marlys had been married a mere four years and already they had two beautiful children, Marlene and Heviathan Junior, and a third on the way.

Whereas that brassy second son of hers, Howell Madison, had to fall in love (that had been his word for it) with that no good prissy little Indella CoraMae Shealy, perpetually stuck at age ten in thinking, actions, and expectations. There was not a single member of the Shealy clan that Momma Cobb could respect. All were nothing but drunks and Saturday night racket makers, only for most of them it did not matter if it was Saturday night or not. How her second son could choose to connect himself with such a crowd she could not understand. But he said he loved Indella and what can a mother do in the face of true love.

But Indella wore on one's patience more than most. Patience was a trait that was difficult for her to manage. Just last night she had had to kick Charlie Billings out of her house. She found him sitting on the living room sofa with her oldest girl, Martha, only sixteen, his hand up her dress and her giving him permission. She found the end of patience as she yelled after the scampering Charlie not to come back again. And Martha had had the brazenness to stand up to Momma Cobb and announce that she intended to become Mrs. Charlie Billings just as soon as he asked her and if he failed to ask her in a timely fashion, then she would ask him. So put that in your pipe and smoke it, the too-big-for-her-britches Martha proclaimed. "Then you can sleep in the chicken coop," Momma Cobb had yelled, "cause I ain't about to let that Charlie step foot inside my house, nor anything of his that he might claim, including you, Miss Fussy!"

That was the temperature in the Cobb household the morning that Indella CoraMae Shealy Cobb came calling with Howbo in his sailor suit and "Sandra Ellen," also known to some as Winnie-Pooh, with pink ribbons in his/her hair.

"What in the name of tarnation is that!" Momma Cobb said without thinking when she saw the newborn. Her crazy daughter-in-law must be pulling a practical joke, that had to be it, was her immediate thought. Because there in front of her, sucking on a pacifier, cheeks decorated with smudged-on rouge, was the most God-awful sight she had ever seen. The baby, now a month old and growing like a weed in an empty pig sty, had been transformed. "He" was a "she" and Momma Cobb had no words to answer when Indella said with smiles from every pore on her face, "Ain't my little Sandra Ellen just the prettiest little thang?"

All Momma Cobb could say was "Good God Awmighty."

And all the smiles from Indella twisted immediately to frowns as she turned herself and her too precious babies around and marched back up the hill from whence she had come to her house beside the railroad tracks.

"You, Indella Shealy," Momma Cobb called after her, "where you thank you're going?"

And Indella said, trying desperately to maintain what little composure was in her, "Home, if you don't mind."

7

There came a tapping at Indella's screen door.

She had just rocked Sandra Ellen to sleep and she did not want her afternoon nap disturbed. Howbo was content playing in the backyard in the wood chip pile. It was her time of day to rest, be herself, not have to worry about bawling babies and changing diapers and cleaning vomit. So Indella meant to sound pissy when she hissed, "Go way, we ain't buying."

"It's me, Della, can I come in?"

Indella recognized Marlys Cobb's voice: sweet, a bit too high-pitched to be normal. "You got your babies with you," she asked.

"Right here on the front porch," Marlys answered.

"I'll come out there then," Indella said slipping through the front screen so it would not make any noise. "How yawl," she asked.

"Fine, real fine," said Marlys. She had pretty little Marlene by the hand and puny little Junior clutched in her left arm.

"Just got the little one pacified," Indella said and grinned. "So yawl wanna come on round back? We can set a spell in the shade."

"Sure is hot, ain't it?" Marlys said as they rounded the side of the house. "That Howbo yonder?" she asked, pointing to the child crawling in the wood chips.

"Bigger'n life," was Indella's snappy response. She glared at her sister-in-law and felt superior. What in the world had Heviathan Cobb seen in this tiny woman, mostly skin and bones, no bosom to speak of even after a couple of kids, no hips, no cheeks on her face and nothing but wide open space between her knees. Heviathan himself, a giant of a man, was more than six feet tall and a belly like he had swallowed a world globe.

"Mind if I put Bubba down, Della? He's grown a ton this last week."

"So how you, Marlene?" Indella asked, poking her finger at the little girl's nose. Oh how she admired that tiny little nose and those rosy cheeks, rosy even without the help of lip-gloss. "I'd let you see my little girl, sweetie, but she's asleep right now in the house. You'll have to come round another time, Okay?"

Marlene was too shy or too dumb or just not ready to say more than "Yessum" to such a suggestion.

"Why don't you go on over there and play with Howbo, Marlene? He's having himself a grand time."

"He do love them wood chips," Indella said. She liked her sister-in-law in spite of the failures on her part. In fact, if the truth be known, Indella liked Marlys because of her failures. She, Indella, loved to feel superior, and Marlys was about the only one around who allowed such feelings, especially now that Indella had her own little girl to show off next to precious little Marlene. "You hear anything from Hev, Marlys?"

"Oh, my, but that fool man done gone and broke his knee cap."

"Well now that's too bad."

"Well not really. Doctors tell him he's gonna heal up all right."

"Well that's good."

"Only the breaks not bad enough to get him sent home."

"Oh now that's rotten luck."

"But it's bad enough to keep him out of harm's way."

"Ain't you the lucky one."

"I feel so. I mean, Howie's where now, Pearl? Some place like that?"

"No, He's still in Norfolk. He don't ship out for another week or two. I got a letter from him yesterday, and he says he may get him a furlough pretty quick."

"That's real good news, Honey."

"Marlene?" Indella said. "I don't think you wanna be throwing them wood chips at Howbo like that. You might poke out one of his eyes."

"Marlene! Behave yourself."

The two teenaged mothers sat in the shade of the post oak tree, Marlys suckling little Junior and sitting on the chopping block and Indella perched on the cross tie of the saw horse Howie had built the year before last. She liked sitting on the saw horse; it made her think of him and the time he took her right there, right out in the open and in the middle of the afternoon. She turned wet just thinking about it. Those days were behind her, not to be repeated, so she feared.

Indella cleared her throat and said with her head tilted in her haughty way, "So, old Heviathan broke his knee cap?"

"Slipped on a wet spot on deck and fell into a gun well."

"What's a gun well?"

"I suspect it's a place where they store all their guns when they ain't using them," Marlys said, ashamed of her ignorance. "Anyway it ain't a bad break, but it's bad enough that he'll be in the infirmary when his ship leaves dry dock."

"He still in Pensacola then?"

"There for a month more at least."

"Maybe Howie'll break his leg before he heads off. Last time he was home, he was talking of being shipped out to fight the Japs. Oh, I hate the idea of my Howie fighting anybody. But them Japs, they got it coming if you ask me."

"So," Marlys whispered, as if afraid somebody might overhear. "You got you a little girl now?"

"My own little Sandra Ellen."

"Got her through adoption, did you?"

"Lord no. Howie and me can't afford to go adopting children. What're you thinking about, honey?"

"So, where'd you get this little girl child?"

"Birthed it," said Indella, filling with superior pride and feelings of grand accomplishments. Then it came to her, this visit was not a normal thing at all. Marlys was on a mission. It was so clear, so obvious. "Why you here, Marlys?" she asked, knowing full well the answer she would get.

"Well--"

"Momma Cobb sent you, didn't she."

"Well--"

"You can tell Momma Cobb she can. . ." She wanted to speak her mind, but she knew better. She did not have the best possible relationship with her mother-in-law and with Howie away at war she never knew when it might become important to keep on her good side.

"She can what, Della?"

"Come calling herself anytime she likes."

"Oh, I know she will."

They sat in silence, listening to the kids playing "root the worms out" in the wood chips. Marlene was carrying on a one-sided conversation with her first cousin, but Howbo, not yet knowing how to shape words, merely grunted or squealed his delight.

Finally, Indella broke the silence. "My Howie got a promotion. He's now carpenter's mate on board the Circe. Ain't that something?"

"How nice. Just what is a carpenter's mate?"

"Heck if I know."

8

It was Saturday morning and Indella was enjoying her sleep. It wasn't often that her two babies left her alone with peace and quiet, but today, somehow or other, they were satisfying themselves and she was reveling in what she liked to call "sleeping in."

Then some blankity-blank busybody banged on her screen door. In the past few days, Howbo had picked up his first clearly understandable word. And once the racket at the front door began, he started yelling, "Momma Mommamamamama."

"Will you hush up? Heaven's sake." Indella was not in the mood to be going to her front door on a hot Saturday morning. No telling who it might be. The landlord? Howie was supposed to have sent the rent through the mail and surely he had not forgotten. The electricity man, maybe. The bulbs had been burning a bit dull lately. Maybe Howie forgot about the electric bill and they were going to cut off all power. Well, what if they did? Indella got along just fine with kerosene lamps for years while living with Glory Bea and she could do it again.

Wham wham wham!

It would not be Glory Bea or Marlys. Neither would be thoughtless enough to come so early on a Saturday morning. Momma Cobb would, though. She would see it as her duty to make certain Indella was up and out of bed at a decent hour and at work tending to her children. Had to be Momma Cobb. Nobody else would dare.

"Who is it?" she said.

"Open the door, woman!"

She knew the voice. She had not heard it in such a long time, but that did not matter. She would recognize it anywhere, anytime. That solid, deep-throated mixture of love and command. Oh my goodness, he had come home!

"Howie?"

"Who else? You gonna let me in?"

Oh, did she let him in! She flung the door so it shook the glasses in the china cabinet and caused Howbo to jump like he had been shot. And there stood Howie, all five foot eight of him, skinny as a lamp post, dressed in his best uniform whites, and grinning like he had caught the golden goose. And she stood frozen, unable to move, to do anything, but gasp for air like a fish on the bottom of the boat.

"You glad to see me or what?" he wanted to know.

And she threw her arms around him and planted her lips against his so tightly that neither could breathe and Howbo stood to the side, gawking. His Momma was acting awful queer and with a total stranger.

Then she pulled away from Howie's grasp, his hands lingering on her private parts and she turned to her son and whispered, "Howbo? You wanna say hello to your papa?"

9

Dinner at Glory Bea's was fried fat back, collard greens from her garden, stewed red potatoes with onions and green peppers, and corn bread and molasses and rhubarb pie for dessert. The same meal her son, Rudy, had been served by Momma Cobb a few years back, so it must be a meal to be remembered. "Delish," Howie said after his third helping of potatoes and greens and finishing half the pie.

Howbo sat on his mother's lap. He did not know what to think about this strange man with the funny looking clothes.

Glory Bea, excused from the table, sat with Winnie-Pooh in the same rocker she had used when Indella was a baby, not that many years ago. Indella knew the dishes were waiting to be washed, but right then, all she wanted was to sit there and stare at her man.

"So, Mister Man," Glory Bea said to Howie Cobb, "how's the Navy treating you?"

"Can't complain," he said, pushing away from the table. "Christ, I'm about to bust."

"Watch your language, young'un," said Glory Bea. "You've got some mighty big e-a-r-s over there, taking in everything you d-o and s-a-y. You home how long this time? Long enough to take a nap?"

"We ship out day after tomorrow."

"Where to?"

"You don't expect them to tell me such stuff as that do you?"

"Why not? You're the carpenter's mate, ain't you?"

Howie smiled. Some big deal that was.

Indella asked, "Just what is it a Carpenter's Mate does?"

"Fix things," he said, stretching and rubbing his stomach. "Glory Bea Shealy, you the best cook this side of Norfolk, Virginia."

"What sorts of things?" Indella pressed.

"Toilet bowls, I betcha," Glory Bea said with a smirk.

"Well, somebody's gotta do it," said Howie. "I fix other things, too, though, like the shelving in the mess, that sort of thing."

"Their toilet bowls are made of wood?" Indella asked.

"I'm not that kind of carpenter, sweetums. I fix whatever they say needs fixing."

"You gonna let me know where you're at once you get there, ain't you?" Said Indella. Howbo had squirmed out of her arms and was crawling into Howie's lap.

"Course," he said. He motioned to Glory Bea. "Brang that bugger to his daddy. Want both my boys, both my fat little buggers right here."

And he cradled them as if he knew what he was doing. He was curious, though, especially about the new one, the one that sucked his thumb even when he was asleep. "How come little Winston's dressed in this pink dress?" he asked.

Indella's face turned a bright pink, almost the color of Winnie-Pooh's ribbons. "Cause it's the only clothes we got, Howie."

"Well, here," he said, taking a roll of bills held together with a rubber band from his pocket and tossing it to his wife. "Go out and get him some decent duds. Don't want folks getting the wrong idea, now do we?" And he chuckled. He didn't see the exchange of looks between Indella and Glory Bea. "Goochie goochie goo," he said, running his finger at Howbo's nose.

"This is a lot of money, Howie."

"Know it. Spend it wisely."

"But where did you get so much--"

"We play poker aboard the Circe. Guess I'm lucky is all."

Glory Bea said, "Lord save us from sinners and gamblers."

Indella's displeasure was even greater than that of Glory Bea's. "You telling me, you gamble, Howell Madison Cobb?"

"It's just poker, that's all."

Glory Bea said, "Got some new prayers what need saying."

Indella didn't know if she should take the wad of money or not. It felt tainted in her hand, like it had Devil-doings all over it. She stuffed it in her pocket anyway, and Howie was pleased. In spite of its taint, the money would be used to meet his family's needs.

"Buy this little critter some manly clothes, Della. Dude him out right."

"You ain't asked after Rudy yet," Indella said.

"You're right," Howie said. Rudy Shealy, the biggest nothing of a human being since his old man, Sylvester, had run away from home right after Pearl, at age sixteen and taken to the rails. Last time Howie had talked to the kid, he had been told things like: "Gonna spend at least one night in every Podunk jail in this country!" and "You ain't lived till you've rode the rods." Of course, Howie had told him: "Done rode the rods and ain't never doing it again." And Rudy had said, "The only way to be free is riding the rails. Being tied to a woman and a passel of kids is no way to live a life." Of course, Rudy had been caught, so he tells it. He was hopping a train in Atlanta when a bull grabbed him by the nape of the neck and lifted him off the ground and said, "Where you think you're heading, bubba?" To which Rudy had said, "To join the Army." To which the bull said, "Then let's do it." The bull had tossed poor Rudy in the back seat of his car and hauled him to the recruiting office and stood there while Rudy signed his name on the dotted line. "Best thing ever happen to me," was how Rudy told it. Even though he was under age at the time, nobody seemed to mind. The army had quotas, and Rudy had helped fill one.

"Rudy's in North Africa, last we heard," Indella said. "That kid wanted to see the world. Well, guess he is."

That was when the front door burst open. That was when Sylvester Shealy, drunker than a dozen skunks downstream of a still, introduced himself into the house with a flourish and a curse.

10

"Should we go home?" Howie asked.

He, his two kids, and Indella sat on Glory Bea's front porch, listening to Sylvester's ranting coming from inside the house. Howie had learned a few years before while he was dating Indella that Sylvester Shealy was not worth a whole hell of a lot when he was drinking, which meant he was not worth a whole hell of a lot any time of night or day. Nearly every time Howie had seen him, Sylvester had been drunk. He did not know where his father-in-law got the money for his liquor, but then maybe that was why Glory Bea took in laundry.

But Sylvester was not all-bad. Far from it. He had a few good points, only Howie could not specify what they might be. Usually, when Sylvester got as drunk as he was this night, he became sickeningly sweet and then he went to sleep. But tonight, his drunk was a mean one. Howie had seen this kind of drunk before, and he knew how to handle it: get as far away from it as he could.

"We can go home in a minute," Indella said. She held Winnie-Pooh close to her breast. "I wanna be sure Momma's gonna be all right."

There was a loud crash from inside as if Sylvester had overturned a cabinet or dumped a drawer of silverware on the floor. "I hate him when he's like this," she said, soft so nobody but Howie would hear.

"Why does Glory Bea put up with it?"

"What else she gonna do? The man's her husband. He's my daddy."

"He's a son of a bitch."

She did not disagree. "You ever been drunk, Howie?"

"Never been drunk a day in my life."

"How about a night?"

"Yeah, once."

"What'd you do?"

"Went to sleep. Woke up the next day with the worst headache I've ever had. That was enough for me. Not touched a drop since."

"You promise me?"

"Not just you. I promise these two growing men boys of ours."

"You're my man," she said, hugging him and putting her head on his shoulder.

Another loud clang came from inside the house, this one like a skillet being tossed against a metal stove.

Howie stood. "Here," he said, "hang onto Howbo for me. Won't be a minute." And he entered the house.

"Hey, bubba," Sylvester said with a huge smile on his face, his mouth full of half-chewed greens. "Nice looking pajamas you wearing there, bud. Look real sharp. Reckon I get me some them?"

Glory Bea was sitting at the table, a wad of collards stuck against the front of her dress and molasses oozing down the side of her face. She stared straight ahead, not acknowledging Howie when he came in the room. The platter that had held the greasy fat back had been smashed against the kitchen door and the jar of molasses, now half empty, sat on the edge of the table, ready to topple into Glory Bea's lap.

"Hey, Bubba," Sylvester said, "care for some cornbread?" And he tossed it. Howie moved aside and let it thud to the floor.

"What does he want here, Glory Bea?" Howie asked, calm and pointed. She was too humiliated to reply.

"I got what I want, sailor boy. So why don't you just go on back to your ship. Care for a shot?" And he offered a bottle that was smudged with grease and stank of beer and wine and whiskey all mixed together.

"I'm talking to Glory Bea," Howie said. He knelt beside her, wiping the goo from the side of her face. "Do you want this drunk in your house, Mrs. Shealy?"

She shook her head, slightly but definitely "No." She whispered, "I kicked him out last week, told him not to come back."

Howie stood. He had faced a drunk once before when he had been sent by Momma Cobb to "The Store" to bring his Uncle Sol home. Sol had no intention of leaving, much less going home. To prove his point, he had drawn a knife and held it menacingly toward Howie and his prime directive from Momma Cobb. Howie learned from Uncle Sol that when a man is drunk, it matters little what he may use as a threat. It is empty, a dare more than anything else. He did not know if Mr. Shealy had a weapon hidden under his shirt, but it made little difference. It was the same situation with Uncle Sol, only now he was older and had the Navy's basic training behind him. He was afraid of no man, regardless of his being drunk or not. He stood, his left foot braced a little behind his right, his right fist balled into a fist. His posture spoke clearly to anyone with a clear head: he would take no crap off any man. "Time for you to be going, Sylvester," he said, politely.

Sylvester laughed. "Big shot," he said. "That's Mr. Shealy to you, Bubba."

Howie said, "That's fine. I can call you anything you like. A snake wants to be called 'Mister,' I can call him 'Mister,' before I cut its head off. From where I'm standing, Mr. Shealy, you got two choices. One--you can go peaceful and nobody gets hurt. Two--you go not so peaceful and I make no promises. Which way do you want it?"

"Jesus. This is my house. Who you thank you are, Bubba? Some sort of Navy god or something?"

"I think I'm sober and I know you're drunk. To my way of thinking, that makes me a little more in charge of my abilities, sir. This house belongs to Mrs. Shealy who's sitting there like a saint. So, which is it? Your choice."

"I think I'll finish my dinner, you don't mind."

"Do mind. Do mind a whole lot, you stinking drunk." And he leaned into Sylvester's face and whispered so Glory Bea couldn't hear, "I don't know about you, Mister Shealy, but I'd sure hate for my sons to see their granddaddy's blood splattered all over this room. So what's it gonna be-- peaceful or not so peaceful?"

Sylvester stood and took several backward steps toward the door. "What's it to you anyway? This is my house, I can come into my own house--"

"When you're sober, maybe. When Mrs. Shealy invites you. But not when you're stinking drunk. Not when you're not invited. I'll give you to three to make up your mind. One--" And he took a threatening step in Sylvester's direction.

"You goddamned son of a--"

"Two."

"You touch me and I swear--"

"Three."

And Sylvester was out the door and into the night. He stopped running when he was two blocks away, and then only to throw up in a ditch.

Howie breathed and relaxed. It had been the same with Uncle Sol: call his bluff and any drunk will go the peaceful route. He turned to Glory Bea who still sat without moving. "He won't bother you any more tonight, Mrs. Shealy."

"That may be," she said. "But where will you be next time?"

"I don't know," he said. And that bothered him. "Maybe there won't be a next time," he said.

She laughed. It wasn't a happy laugh at all.

11

Sunday morning, Howie woke early, took his shower, kissed his wife and kids good-bye, and headed for the highway, his duffel over his right shoulder, and he did not look back. If he looked back, he would turn around and stay and the hell with Uncle Sam's damn Navy.

So he kept walking, out to Highway 78, and hung his thumb out, hoping for a lift all the way north to Norfolk. If he was lucky, he would make it by six tomorrow, else he would be AWOL and for that he might as well stay home.

After Howie had disappeared around the corner, Indella counted the money he had given her. She nearly fainted. She had never seen so many big bills in one place at one time. Heavens, with this much money, she could outfit an entire shipload of kids.

She put Howbo in his best sailor suit and combed his hair and tied his shoes. She then dressed Winston in her very best pink sundress, smeared rouge on her cheeks, and tied a ribbon around her head. She stepped back from the two and grinned. "I swanny," she said with a nod to her head. "If you two ain't the prettiest boy and girl children I ever laid eyes on."

And that's the way she left the house that beautiful sunlit Sunday morning, with Howbo by the hand and Sandra Ellen in the stroller, eager to share the treasures of her life with everyone she met in the Village that day.

As she pushed the stroller down the sidewalk toward Liberty Baptist Church, she said a prayer under her breath, something like "Dear Lord, be with my hubby cause he's the only one I got."

"Where you headed, swabbie?" the old man with a
wart beside his nose asks as you get in the rattly old Ford
pick-up truck.

"Norfolk," you say.

"Why Norfolk's the other direction," the old man says.
"You done got yourself turned around, sonny."

"No shit."

*"I wouldn't lie to a man in the service. You bet,
Norfolk's a good fifty miles other direction."*

"You best let me out, then, sir, you don't mind."

*"Nothing to worry about, son. I gather from your get-
up you're bound for the Navy yard in Norfolk. I'll get you
there, good as you please."*

*And he turns the old pickup around in the road. "I got
me a son in the Navy myself,"* he says. *"He's assigned to
the Franklin. You wouldn't be from the Franklin, would
you?"*

"The Circe, sir."

"That right? What's the Circe? A battlewagon?"

"Cargo ship. Brand spanking new."

"That right?" You ride in silence for a second or two.
"Now the Franklin," the man says, *"is one big hunk of
ship. But the Circe, what's she like? A match box? Heh,
heh heh?"*

*You say nothing. You have nothing to say. Yeah, a
match box. When you first put foot aboard the Circe, you
thought: Be Jesus, this thing's huge! That was before you
got an eyeful of some of those other ships: the Franklin, the
New Mexico, and the Wasp. Even some of the LST's they're
building these days make the Circe seem awful puny. But
then you're glad in your own way. Let's say they ship you
out and you find yourself in a real mixer and bombs are
being tossed here and about and torpedoes are going every
which way, then you'll be glad that the Circe's just a puny
little thing, hardly worth the effort. Maybe it'll be the size*

of the ship that'll get you home safe and sound to wife and kids. You pray something will.

Shipping out. That's what your buddies are doing even now. You're late, Howie Cobb. So what's new in that? They won't weigh anchor until every last one of you's aboard. Will they? You're supposed to have been there by six and it's already past seven. Lord knows what kind of trouble you're gonna be in when you finally get to dry dock. Head's gonna roll, no doubt about that. And here you are, in the slowest damn Ford pick-up truck God ever poured gasoline into. What're you gonna do? Hell, nothing to do but go along with the ride and take what comes when it comes. But Lord knows, the skipper ain't gonna be too pleased, not with you showing up like this.

So you sit back, close your eyes and let the man with the wart beside his nose chatter on while you relish the goodness your precious Indella represents. What a day it was when you first put eyes on her.

CHAPTER TWO
How Indella Coramae Shealy Met howell Madison Cobb

1

Four teenaged boys strolled down Fairburn Highway tossing a heavily taped wad of string they called a baseball, reliving highlights of the game they had just won over in the Hunnicutt pasture, defeating a bunch of dirt farmers from McWorter. It took the oldest of the Hembree boys, the lankiest and most world-aware kid of the bunch, to notice the black-haired, black-eyed girl, skinny, not yet fully formed, reading a book on the porch steps of her whitewashed clapboard house.

It was hot. The girl watched the four full-of-themselves ball players from behind the safety of her book as she fanned herself and pretended to read. She acted surprised when she heard the first whistle. It was lewd and sassy, the kind she had heard her daddy, Sylvester Shealy, use dozens of times when a good-looking woman passed by the house. She straightened her jumper with the second whistle, an even sassier sound than the first. This was followed by a leering laugh that Glory Bea would have called "Dirty minded, typical of anything that wears pants."

The four teenagers had stopped near the fence that guarded the entrance to the Shealy place. Three of them leaned against the front fence post that had trouble sustaining the weight of its gate, and was not prepared to hold the leanings of healthy young men from Douglasville. The fence creaked and sagged as three of them gaped open-mouthed at the girl's long black hair and her olive-toned skin. They were full to overflow with baseball and winning and homeruns and cow patties fresh as daisies after a spring rain. It did not matter to them that the female they ogled was too young to be treated in such a way.

The fourth in the group stood in the middle of the road, embarrassed it seemed, obviously wanting to continue the winning march home. He did not like being around the Hembree brothers when they were in their sassy moods. Nor did he care for the sounds they made with the saliva in their mouths. It bothered him that his own brother joined in the way he did, slapping the boards of the front fence with his open palm and whistling through his teeth like some hick from the hills. The fourth boy wanted to get back to the Village and share the glory of his pasture-ball exploits with anybody willing to listen. After all, two unassisted double plays and four-for-four were worth a lot of cockadoodling around the supper table.

"What do they want?" Rudy, the girl's brother, asked from behind her shoulder. "Bunch of Village hoods, betcha," he whispered, his flip-staff in hand, ready with a smooth creek stone. He had not as yet been called on to use the weapon against anything but birds and a rabbit or two, but he was practiced. He was primed to protect his sister, if needed.

"You boys run on," the girl yelled.

The fourth boy tugged at the shirtsleeves of the others. "Let's get going," he said to the Hembree boys who were doing most of the whistling and ogling and making of vulgar sounds.

"You don't get on, I'll call my Papa," the girl threatened, clutching the book against her chest.

"You don't got a papa," the oldest Hembree said and laughed. He was the brassy one, not ashamed to say whatever came into his head. Besides, he was right, in a way, about the girl and her father. He said, "This is the Shealy place. I know old Sylvester Shealy, a sot if I ever saw one. He don't live here except when it's convenient."

"Come on fellas," the fourth said, "leave her alone."

"You got pretty hair," the other Hembree lad said and sniggered. Glory Bea would have called him a no-good underside of a mushroom if she had heard his and his brother's sneers, and she would probably have been right. He insinuated more with the twist of his mouth than with the tone of his voice, "Where'd you get such pretty hair?"

"God's gift," she answered. That was not the thing to say. Now, even the third boy laughed and pointed. Only the fourth stood aside, slipping more and more away from the others. This was not his means of doing things, taunting young girls from the road like this.

"You boys go on," she yelled.

"One of these days, she's gonna be a looker," the sassy Hembree said loud enough for everyone to hear, even the girl. Then they sauntered down the road, the fourth holding back, keeping a distance from the idiots he considered more embarrassments than friends.

Besides he wanted one last look at this girl he had not seen before. She struck him as somebody he might like to get to know, give her a few years. Anybody who would sit around on a beautiful Saturday afternoon with her nose in a book had to have something going for her. Being a bookworm and being a female were not bad things to be, he estimated. In fact, the two almost went together and made something totally new and maybe even precious: a female worthy of his attention. The thing he did not know was that she was not reading at all. She was using the book as a way to hide the small hand mirror she was using to admire her face and hair.

She followed as far as the gate, watching the boys, then into the road, watching them, then to the edge of the field, hoping the fourth one, the one lagging behind, would turn around and come back and smile at her. He was the handsomest boy she had ever seen. She wanted to stare into his eyes and memorize everything about him. She did not understand it at the time, but this boy, whoever he might be, was somebody she really wanted to know intimately.

He stopped just before the bend in the Fairburn Highway where the scrubby plum trees hid the Shealy place from the rest of the world. He paused, looked over his shoulder, and sort of waved. She could not be sure, but it faintly resembled a wave. At least his hand moved from his overall pocket and a smile nearly broke from his serious mouth.

"What's your name?" she yelled.

"Howie. Howell Madison Cobb," he called back. "Remember that cause I'm gonna be famous! What's yours?"

"Indella CoraMae Shealy," she answered.

He waited for a bit before he turned the bend and disappeared from sight.

Indella had an urge to tag along, search his face and maybe even touch it, find out what he was expecting to be famous at, how he was going to go about finding fame and fortune in this part of Georgia in these depression times, anything. Just hear his voice and be close enough to study his eyes. She did not give in to it, this urge, but it was strong, stronger than most anything she had felt in longer than she could remember. She resisted. Instead, she returned to her porch and her mirror and her pestering brother.

"What did he say?" Rudy wanted to know.

"Stop bothering me," she said, taking her book with her into the clapboard house. She let the screen door slam behind her, punctuating her attitude toward her younger brother.

Rudy took a shot at the mailbox with his flip-staff and clipped it with a rough-edged stone. His aim was getting better. Soon he would be able to protect his sister, his mother, the clapboard house, anything, if that protection were ever needed, which he secretly hoped it would. Maybe next time Sylvester came home, stinking of home brew, he would be ready, flip in hand.

Glory Bea worked at the sink in the kitchen, her forearms stained yellow from the bucket of dye she was using to color flour sacks. The scowl on her face was etched so deeply it did not disappear even when she smiled, which was not often.

"Momma?" Indella said. "Do you know anybody by the name of Cobb?"

"Go on, child. That's the most commonest name there is."

"Not as common as Shealy."

"Shows what you know. There's a whole passel of folks by the name of Cobb lives over in the Village," she said. The dyeing had to be done if she was to sew the cloth into shirts. Shirts had to be made if she was to sell them in the Village for whatever she could get for them: food preferably, but just about anything would do.

"You know any of them Cobbs?"

"Will you leave me to this, Indella? Go outside and pesk with your brother."

The girl stopped at the door; the book clasped to her flat chest, the mirror carefully concealed inside. What she had under her jumper that was nearly too small for her to notice was a sudden embarrassment. Though she wore one, there was nothing inside her brassiere, an undergarment she secured from her Aunt Azzie in the Village who knew about such things and was not afraid, like Glory Bea, to talk about them. There was no reason to wear the weak excuse of a brassiere except that other girls her age wore them. But with nothing for the undergarment to hold, it was an irritant to her skin. Why did she not have breasts like her friends? She did not ask her mother, though she wanted to. She asked her Aunt Azzie who laughed at her and said, "Patience, patience, patience." But Indella was running out of patience. Why did boys, like those four in the road, have to make fun of her? She was already a teenager, almost grown. It was time to have boys find her pretty--

A looker. That was what one of the boys had said. She was going to be a looker someday--his words. When would that day come? She leaned against the doorjamb and ran her fingers across her hair as if discovering for the first time that the black mass was hers and had beauty in it. "Do you thank I'm pretty, Momma?" she asked.

"Oh, for heaven's sake."

"I wouldn't mind being a looker. I think it might be fun, being a looker. And getting married. Have a handsome, sweet, caring husband. . . like Howie Cobb." She whispered his name over and over, "Howell Madison Cobb."

"All men're the same, Button. Not worth the time it takes to collect enough spit to spray them with.".

"Howie Cobb's worth it."

"If this Howie Cobb, whoever he is, has got himself a set of testicles, he ain't worth the time of day."

Indella thought about it and decided not to ask. She was not sure what testicles were, and whatever they might be, she was certain that if Howie Cobb had them, she could help him get rid of them. So in spite of her better judgment, her thought came pouring out of her mouth, unprotected, untested: "Howie Cobb's the man I'm gonna marry."

Glory Bea dripped yellow dye on the linoleum as she turned toward her still-too-young daughter. "What on earth are you talking about?"

The thought felt right inside Indella's head. She liked the way the notion eased into her mind, almost unquestioned. Anything so simple and easy must be the will of the Lord. So she kept the idea where it was and almost gloated with the pleasure such thinking gave her. "I'm gonna marry that boy, Momma. Him and me are gonna be so very happy."

"Now which boy is that may I ask?"

"Why, Howell Madison Cobb." Her eyes were clear, it was so obvious, so natural. "Mrs. Howell Madison Cobb." Of course, that was the way it was to be. "Indella Shealy Cobb." Perfect. She would have to practice writing it over and over to make it look just right. "Mrs. Indella Cobb, wife of Howell Madison Cobb of Douglasville, Georgia." Everything about it was perfect. Almost beautiful. It frightened her, it was so easy.

Glory Bea dried her hands on her apron leaving yellow stains on top of grease. "You are so full of yourself, Miss Pris. I swear, you and Rudy are going to be the death of me yet. . . if Sylvester don't do me in first."

And sure enough, Sylvester showed up that night. He smelled his normal self and acted it. The little clapboard house set back from the road was not big enough on Saturday nights when Sylvester came home reeking of rotgut and barbecue. Indella locked herself in her room so he could not get to her like he had too many times before, and Rudy had hid in the hall closet. His cot in the front room did not have a lock on it. He refused to come out of the closet even when Sylvester tempted him with a chocolate-covered cherry. Rudy knew there was no chocolate-covered cherry. The clothes in the closet smelled of mothballs. Smelled a sight better than Sylvester, so Rudy did not mind. Someday, he promised himself, he would get drunk as Sylvester and bust his daddy's head open with a fence post. And nobody would blame him. Cause he would be drunk.

Indella covered herself with quilts and listened to Sylvester's curses coming through the thin walls. He wanted to spend most of his time in the bedroom with her Momma. Glory Bea's little cries of pain hurt Indella. This night, they were not anything extraordinary. Little cries that came out of Glory Bea involuntarily. There was nothing for show in Glory Bea's crying, nothing to attract attention. They were simply there, part of spending time with Sylvester in his wicked state on Saturday nights. Then quiet. Sylvester had fallen asleep. When he came home stinking, sleep for him was not that far away. On such nights, sleep seldom came to anybody else in the house. Indella wanted to find her Momma and give her a hug, but she knew better. She even wanted to give Rudy some comfort, but she stayed put. Safer that way.

Come morning, Indella knew her Momma would be bruised around the eyes and neck and probably other places, but she would never see those marks. Glory Bea wore long-sleeved cotton dresses following Sylvester's visits, regardless of the heat outside. Indella noticed this but did not say anything. She understood. The couple of times Sylvester had gotten to her caused Glory Bea to dress Indella in long-sleeves, too. She wondered: would Howell Madison Cobb be another Sylvester Shealy? Would she have to wear long-sleeved dresses to church on Sunday morning like Glory Bea? Would she love him anyway, if he did?

In the books she read men were different from what she saw in her own house. In books, men came home from work every night and treated their women with tenderness. Women in the books never had welts on their necks or blood on their pillows after Saturday nights. And men did not have the stink of alcohol on them when they came into the house. In the books, men were as wonderful as women were if not more so. Most of them, anyway. Sometimes, there was a Sylvester, but usually he got what was coming to him one way or another. Maybe that was something she could pray for, a man like the ones in the books who made rescues and wore shining armor and rode white horses. Maybe if she prayed hard enough and long enough, that man would come home on Saturday night and make all of them feel good.

God must not attend to the prayers of fourteen-year-old girls, because Sylvester did not change. So, she tried a different prayer. Let Howie Cobb be like the men she read about. Let him not be like the rest of them. Instead, dear Lord, she prayed, grant him the qualities she longed for. Wrap him up like an Ivanhoe or a Little Minister. She knew deep inside Howie had to be the perfect man. How else could she love him so?

2

Rudy Shealy wandered throughout the Village. He was looking for somebody, he told Indella, somebody special. His sister scoffed. The scruffy-nosed little brat could not find a pinecone in the woods if it fell on his head. "Doing something good, just for you," he told her. And she sneered. But he was gone, nonetheless, three days running, scouring the Village from one end to the next. It was what he did best: wandering.

"I don't like you going so far from home," Glory Bea said to her only son. "Stay closer or I'll whip you good."

He gave no attention to her concerns. The third day, he turned to asking for help. "I'm looking for a fellow named Howie Cobb," he said half a dozen times, and each time he was pointed a little deeper into the Village.

A once-upon-a-time-whitewashed slat house sitting in the midst of a grassless yard and shaded by a scrubby oak tree with most of its roots above ground, the same as every other small village house, was where he was pointed last. The yard was cluttered with piles of raked leaves and limbs, a few broken toy trucks, the tattered remains of what had once been a rag doll, and a rusted metal recliner chair that had a quilt remnant in the seat. The floor of the porch creaked as he walked across it. The front door was open but the screen was latched.

He knocked.

No answer.

The screen door was decorated with a patch of cotton and small tangle of tin can rattles. He knocked a second time a bit harder, making the tin cans clatter against one another. A boy about a head taller than Rudy stared through the rusty screen.

"Hey," the boy said.

"Hey yourself," was all Rudy could think to say back.

"I'm Pierson Cobb. Who're you?"

"Rudolph Shealy," Rudy said. He hated his full name--sounded like a sissy pants. He didn't know why he used it in answering Pierson. He seldom let anybody else use it. Maybe it was because this other kid was lumbered with a name like Pierson that had yanked Rudolph out of him. He did not have time to think much about it before Pierson unlatched the screen door and pulled him inside.

The house smelled of fat back and collard greens. The rich, salty aroma created a rumble inside Rudy and drew him deeper into the dark house. He followed Pierson down the hallway past what had to be bedrooms for half a dozen kids to the back part of the house and the kitchen.

"We're having dinner. You hungry?" Pierson asked.

"A little," he said. Rudy did not know how to say "No" to food. His round pudgy face and full tight belly were evidence.

Rudy grinned. He liked what he saw. At the head of the long, oilcloth covered wooden table sat Alexander Stevens Cobb. The man was second cousin to a leprechaun. Indella had read to him of the friendly creatures and here was one in the flesh, feeding cornbread and collard greens into his mouth. The Leprechaun was flanked by kids of every age. Rudy knew Martha--he went to school with her--and she grinned and waved at him across the table and slid her chair to one side, making room for him. The others stopped their chewing and stared.

"Who's your friend, Pierson?" Momma Cobb, the woman at the stove, asked. She wore clothes like his Momma's and her hair was the same, only a little grayer, and maybe there were a few more wrinkles around her eyes that hid behind a pair of bifocals with tortoise shell rims.

"That's Rudy," Martha said. She blustered with the pride of knowing and took the kick Abbie, sitting to her right, gave her under the table.

Pierson pulled a chair beside his place at the table and shoved his older brother, Hev, aside. Heviathan was tall and lean with a handsome square freckled face. He said he was finished anyway and left the table to stand near the back door where a cool breeze felt good. Hev was the best looking of the five Cobb boys gathered in the cramped kitchen, but he did not seem to know it. He picked his teeth with a sliver he pulled from the top of the pine-slab doorjamb.

Momma Cobb put a plate of cornbread, collards, and fat back in front of Rudy and slid the container of sorghum next to his plate. "Eat," she said.

He ate.

Martha giggled as she whispered something to her sister, Abbie. Rudy admired the third sister, younger than him, sitting beside the Leprechaun at the end of the table.

She was silent, solemn, and sincere, not giggly like her two older sisters.

"That's Brenda," Pierson said, noting his new buddy's gaze. "She's next to the baby. The baby's him," and he pointed to Horatio, at most three years old. "Say hey to Rudolph, Horatio." And the youngest threw a collard green at Pierson's head.

Pierson pointed around the table. "That's Hank and Martha--"

"We go to school together," said Martha.

"--And Abbie and Howie and Daddy and Momma and that's Hev standing in the door and that's us."

It was Howie Rudy stared at now. Howie at first ignored him, then punched Hank in the side and pointed, "The kid's got bug eyes!" They laughed.

"So," Momma Cobb said, finally taking her own chair at the table. "What brangs you to our house, young man?"

Rudy swallowed the chewed-on chunk of cornbread he had in his mouth, looked about the table from one bright face to the next, and finally pointed a finger at Howie.

Howie leaned back in his chair and laughed. "I don't know you, squirt."

"I know it. But I've been looking all over for you. Took me three days to find you. My Momma's worried sick about me being over here in this part of town."

"What do you want with Howie?" asked Hev. He was mild mannered and easy going, not like his younger brother Hank who kicked at Howie under the table and caused the water glasses to clatter.

"I come to tell him something."

"What's your last name, son?" asked the Leprechaun.

"Shealy, sir."

"Shealy. They some Shealys over across the tracks. Sylvester. You kin to Sylvester Shealy, son?"

"He's my papa."

"Hmmm," said Alexander Stevens. "Too bad." He shook his head and left the table. "Good food, May Lou," he called as he wandered from the kitchen. Rudy marveled that the Leprechaun was not much taller when he stood. He had to be part midget.

Momma Cobb looked at the child across the table and shook her head. "Sylvester Shealy. A sad thing, this life," she said as she ate her portion of collard greens. "You just eat all you want," she said.

"Why? What's wrong with his daddy?" Pierson wanted to know.

"Shush, you idjit," said Hev from the door.

"My papa left us about a year ago," Rudy said. He was not used to lying, and he knew Glory Bea would belt him if she knew he was lying now. He cast his eyes down in humility. He was not ashamed. It was simply the gesture he had seen his Momma and sister use time and again when Sylvester's name was brought up.

"Left you for what?" asked Hank. "Another family?"

"Button it," Howie said, poking Hank in the ear.

"From the looks of him, I can understand why!" said Hank.

Sniggers grew out of Martha, Abbie, Pierson, and even Brenda.

"Leave me alone," warned Rudy. The hairs behind his collar were ready to bristle, the thin muscles in his upper arms tightened. He stuffed a wedge of sorghum-soaked cornbread in his mouth and munched on it.

"What do you want with me?" asked Howie. But Rudy's mouth was too full to say anything right away.

"He wants you to go find his papa for him, Howell," Hank said. And he slapped his brother's head with a dishtowel.

"He wants you to shut up, Hank," Martha said, ready to defend her schoolmate if necessary.

"I got a message for Howie Cobb from my sister," Rudy blurted out.

Howie's mouth dropped open. "I don't know your sister."

"Maybe not, but she knows you. And she says--"

All ears, even Momma Cobb's from the kitchen sink where she was dipping water from a metal pail over the dirty dishes, turned to Rudy. He flushed with embarrassment. Indella had not asked him to do this. He had volunteered to find Howie Cobb. If she knew, she would most likely kill him with a brick upside the head. He caught Brenda's eye, and she seemed to say in her silent, reassuring way, "Don't worry, nobody's gonna hurt you, not right away anyhow."

"Go on," Hev urged.

Rudy swallowed hard. He had no experience with such things. He did not know if Howie or one of his brothers would squash him like a bug when he said what he had to say. But he had come this far. There was no turning back now. "My sister," he said, "claims she's gonna marry you, Howie Cobb."

Even Momma Cobb joined in the fun. Alexander Stevens came in from the sitting room, snuff cup in one hand, Bible in the other, and said, "What in the world's going on?"

"Howie is getting married!" Came a chorus of voices. Howie had to flee through the front door, slamming it behind him, to get away from the taunts.

After that, Rudy Shealy was a welcomed comrade for Hank and Pierson. They recognized a kindred spirit when they met one.

And maybe, Rudy thought, maybe if he hung around long enough he would get a chance to say something clever to Brenda, maybe impress her in some way he did not know.

3

The first time Howell Madison Cobb saw Indella CoraMae Shealy as somebody other than a bookworm was two weeks later. At the beginning, Howie laughed off the snide remarks about him and his forthcoming marriage to the Shealy girl. It was a little funny, and a whole lot embarrassing. After all, he was a seventeen-year-old man, and she was just barely a teenager. What would folks in the Village think about him if they ever took the rumors (which were spreading faster than the mumps) to be true? After two weeks of questions from friends, relatives, neighbors, and even strangers about his forthcoming nuptials, Howie decided time had come to put an end to the entire shebang once and for all. No matter how often he said: "There's nothing to it, folks" nobody seemed to listen.

The only way he knew to put something like this behind him was to find the girl, confront her, and deny the rumors to her face if necessary. And witnessed, too, by God, and get all this marriage business behind him. Besides, there was Carol Bauman who was paying him a lot of attention at church these days. Sitting with him when she could, even holding his hand under cover of the hymnal, and the Statum twins. Both of whom he could court with no trouble whatsoever, and Hev's fiancée, Marlys Abbrams, had a sister, Lacy, cute as could be who was an old woman compared to this Shealy girl--Lacy was all of fifteen and "Ready-For-Freddie," according to Hev. At any rate, it was time, past time even, to put this marriage mess in its rightful place.

Rudy was over at the Cobb place a good deal those days, finding Hank's company of particular interest. So, one afternoon after he got off the cotton-thread shift at the mill, Howie followed Rudy home with Pierson along for

witness. Since Hev refused, being too infatuated with
Marlys to have anything to do with his younger brother's
marital problems, especially now that Hev and Marlys were
talking along those lines themselves.

Howie and Pierson stood outside the fence as Rudy
rushed up to the house and disappeared inside. They
fidgeted. Howie plucked a straw from the sagebrush
growing around one of the posts and used it to pick his
teeth. The field across the way had sprouted cotton and
was etched a deep green against the far row of trees and the
redness of the soil.

Rudy returned. "She ain't coming out," he called to
the two brothers at the fence.

"So why not?"

"She just ain't," said Rudy as he sauntered to the fence
and hung against it by standing on the lower board. "She's
a girl. Who ever heard of a girl acting right?"

And Pierson nodded. He was thinking of Martha and
Abbie and Brenda and the half dozen girls around his house
all the time. "Girls are pains in the boom booms," he said.

"You want to see my place?" Rudy asked his friend.

"What place?"

"The wildcat den. Its back behind the house." The
two younger boys scooted out of sight before Howie could
stop them.

He paced for a bit in front of the house. He could
leave. He should. He had made this effort, but she was not
gracious enough to honor it. Well, forget her. Her and all
girls like her. She wanted to marry him? Well, hell could
freeze over and the heavens melt, and he would still be his
own man, his and nobody else's. Not even Carol Bauman's
for God's sake. She had actually kissed him a few nights
earlier in the darkened parking lot of the church.

The stone he threw at the row of mailboxes clattered
against the first and put a small dent in the metal. He was

startled he had hit something and felt as if he should apologize to somebody for putting a dinger in the box.

"Do you want something?"

Indella was standing on the front porch, dressed in a pink print dress, a pink bow in her black hair, and new saddle oxfords on her feet. This girl is only fourteen? My God, he thought, she looks older than me.

"You get in this house, young lady," he heard her Momma call from inside. But Indella ignored Glory Bea and sat on the top step, clasping her legs together at the knees and hugging them as if to keep them from knocking together. Sitting there, like that, he remembered her from before, the girl with the book and the long lingering stares. That was weeks ago. She was just a kid then. Now, she looked like she had grown up. An Almost Woman.

"Hi," Howie said across the fence.

"Rudy said you wanted to talk to me."

"Well. . ."

Glory Bea stood in the door. She had a leather strap wrapped around her right wrist, ready for whatever might be the young man's intention. "You're too old for my girl, you hear me? You just be on your way. Go on home now."

"Get inside the house, Momma."

"Indella, I'm not about to let you--"

"Go inside. I'll take care of this."

If motherly looks could kill, Howie was dead ten times over. But Glory Bea turned on her heels and slammed the screen door behind her, almost causing the piece of cotton to fly off. She muttered as she went, "I don't know where they get their ideas these days."

"Care to set with me on the porch?" called Indella.

"I ain't done nothing to your Momma," he said.

"I know. Come on over and set a spell."

"I don't take to women with straps in their hands," said Howie as he edged through the gate and down the path lined with tulips and red bricks. "My name's Howie Cobb--"

"I know who you are."

"So I hear."

"You're sixteen--"

"Seventeen."

"Seventeen, work in the cotton mill, have four brothers and three sisters and you're not even Catholic, your daddy's a preacher at Liberty Baptist but he works in the cotton mill, too, and so does your Momma and older brother. His name is Heviathan, they call him Hev for short, and he's in love with a girl name of Marlys Abbrams, good friend of mine. You've been seeing a girl named Carol Bauman--"

"Now wait a minute."

"But that's okay by me. You'll get over her. You live in the Village. You love baseball and are a pretty good shortstop, I guess, don't really know what that is. You dropped out of school after the third grade to help support your family, and you're about the best looking man I've ever set eyes on."

"How do you know all this?"

"Is any of it wrong?"

"You've been talking about me to other folk?"

"I have the right. After all, I've decided I'm going to marry you."

"Now, damn it--"

"Don't you swear in my front yard, young man!" Glory Bea yelled from inside the house.

"You want to go for a walk? " Indella asked.

He stammered. He did not know this girl and she did not know him, though she seemed to have some pretty impressive facts about him. And there he was looking at her and liking what he saw, listening to her threats of marriage and not taking flight like something inside him said he should. She smelled good. She had eyes that sliced through his defenses and left him dangling like so much ham in the smokehouse. And her touch, she had placed a tentative hand on his arm when she asked about taking a walk, was soft as a bee wing on an azalea bloom. It sent sparklers through him and made his blood rush about without reason.

"Sure," he said. Stupid fool idiot, something inside his head said. You better get out of this. Quick.

"If you leave the yard, I'm calling your daddy," Glory Bea yelled from the house.

"We don't have a telephone," Indella whispered as they stepped through the gate and into the road. "She knows we're getting married. She'll get used to the idea."

You love her smell. Like orange marmalade mixed with crushed chinaberries. Her smell rushes into your crotch and causes your John Henry to swell and do its pulsing thing. Uncomfortable, but it sure as hell feels good, that pulse, that heartbeat. Your Momma would call it lust, but you don't care, it feels too good to care.

Your knuckles brush as you stroll down the dusty road. You can't be sure, but she's allowing her hand to be touched. It's what she wants. Contact. And you love the feel of her skin against yours.

You start by telling her that you've no intention of marrying, not now, not ever, that you've got things to do and places to go and sights to see. You tell her the truth, that God hadn't made you to be the marrying kind, that you know down in the depths of your soul that you weren't intended to be a family man. That getting married would be the worst choice you could possibly make that all you would do would make a whole bunch of people unhappy. You didn't know these things about yourself, but they are the truth. Truth hurts, you see this immediately as tears swarm down her beautiful cheeks. 'Now don't do that', you want to say but can't and you don't know why. You offer her the sleeve of your shirt and she whisks the tears away, her smile, that magnificent smile that you figure is the result of days of practice, replaces them.

"Don't you think I'm pretty?" she asks and you know the answer: YES, the prettiest female on God's green earth. You could spend a week staring at her face and not grow tired of it. But marriage?

You stop in the road and turn to her. It's time, past time to bring all this business to an end. You've got your life to live and no beautiful, alluring, temptress of a female is going to keep you from living it the way you choose. She stands in front of you, smiling, tears in her eyes, leaning towards you in that way, that special way that comes from being a woman. And you lean, too, towards that tempting mouth, those perfect lips. . . which touch, gently, softly, and you're pulling her to you the way you've seen them do in motion pictures and her body is against yours, her head turned up to you, giving itself, body, soul, all of it to you and you accept it. Your defenses are gone. Your newly acquired self-awareness is gone. Your determination to live your life the way you choose is gone. Your dream of the future is gone. And in its place is a new dream, one you don't resist because, suddenly, it is so right, so absolutely right, even though it may not be for you, that there is no way under God's sun and moon that you can say no to it.

"So. . ." the words slip out of you and you don't know why. All you know is this young girl has suddenly become incredibly important to you, more important even than the fact that all you can promise her is a life of unhappiness. "When?"

"When?"

"Married?"

She whispers in an embarrassed way, "I'll marry you when I turn sixteen, not a day sooner. I'll be sixteen in two years."

Two years.

You'll be nineteen, almost twenty, an old man. You aren't sure you can wait that long. But you say, your good sense leaving you for all time, "Okay."

CHAPTER THREE
Howie Cobb And Indella Coramae Shealy Are Married

1

"They love each other," Alexander Stevens Cobb said. He was in bed with his wife of thirty-five years. Usually when Momma Cobb said something it was the law. But when she said "I WON'T HAVE NO SON OF MINE MARRYING INTO THAT SHEALY CLAN!!" for everyone in the entire Village to hear, the Leprechaun had spat into his snuff cup and waited his time. He knew he would have the chance to get his thoughts organized for May Lou to hear.

"What does love have to do with anything?" she wanted to know.

"Well, it's the new thing. Love and marriage. They go together, you know that. It says in Leviticus--"

"Don't go quoting scripture to me, old man. When did you turn all lovey-dovey anyway?"

"When I first met you."

"Oh, get on with you. You never loved me and you know it."

"Do so. Did and do. That first time I put eye on you, I had a soft spot, right here, and it's been there ever since."

"You're nothing but one big soft spot, Papa. That I know for a fact."

"If I am, it's 'cause of you, sweetums."

And there was blush in Momma Cobb's voice as she whispered, "Get on with you." They were quiet for a moment before she spoke again. "We can't afford no formal wedding."

"Question is, can we afford not to afford one? Those kids, they're gonna get married, come hell or high water."

"You don't suppose she's. . ."

"Now, May Lou, where do you get these ideas. That young thing's as God fearing as you and me put together. There's no way--"

"Still, she's a Shealy. You know about them Shealys."

"Yes, and I know you, too. You're not the one to go around blaming on offspring the sins of the parents. Jesus himself spoke on the subject. 'Judge not that you be not judged,' John--"

"Well, as far as I'm concerned, if Howie's dead set on this marriage, he can take care of things on his own. We're in no position to be of any help, even if we were of a mind to lend a hand."

"You gonna tell him that?"

"He'll just have to figure it out for himself."

"It's good having him home, though, ain't it?"

"Good having him home."

"The CCC's made a man of him. Strong, healthy."

"They didn't put the fear of the Lord in him." Momma Cobb had been trying to get her second son baptized for years, to no avail, even though Howie had come home from his year in the C's claiming to have found Jesus. "Where?" his mother had asked, and he had said, "On a mountain side in the Black Hills." And she had not questioned him because she had not wanted to know.

"You're gonna push them young folks to take drastic steps, May Lou."

"You mean, they gonna run off and do it on the sly?"

"Sure thing."

"Well," she said, patting her man on the top of his head. "It was good enough for us, should be good enough for them."

They were quiet for a moment or two. The dark of the house settled over them and the backbreaking work at the mill called them to sleep. Alexander Stevens whispered, "Which way you going?"

"Front to you."

"All right," he said and turned with his back to his wife and she snuggled against him, their arms interlocked. Alexander Stevens sighed, it felt so good. "Now, this," he said in nothing more than a whisper, "is love."

2

On a Saturday morning in early August, instead of piling into Hev's third hand Chevrolet coupe and heading off to the Hunnicutt's pasture on Fairburn Highway for their usual game of ball, Howie, Indella, Hev, and Marlys drove north to Ringgold, a place noted throughout the state for quickie marriages and divorces. "No questions asked, all problems solved. No couple denied and may the good Lord bless you and keep you, amen." By twelve-oh-five that afternoon, Howie was kissing his very own wife and Indella was letting herself be kissed while making plans, first a boy and then a girl.

"So, what're you gonna tell Momma?" Hev asked as he treated the newlyweds to an ice cream cone in downtown Ringgold.

"The truth, I guess. Wouldn't know what else to tell her," was Howie's answer.

"She ain't gonna like it."

"She don't have to. It ain't her that's newly married. Glory Bea's gonna let us live in her spare room until we can find something better."

"Oh my goodness," squealed Marlys. Everybody thought she had dropped her ice cream down her dress front. Instead, she gave Indella the biggest hug yet. "I just realized," she said. "Married in August, first baby in May. And May, everybody knows, is the best month of them all to be born in. Why, a May baby's blessed by the moon with good luck and the sun with long life. Ain't you just the luckiest two people in the whole wide world?"

Howie swallowed hard. He had not planned on starting a family quite so soon. But the look in Indella's eye told him he had better start thinking that way, else there would be trouble in his future.

"Let's go on a honeymoon," Indella said, rushing her tongue over the cone to keep ice cream from dripping on her skirt.

"Me and Marlys got to get home to Marlene," Hev said. "Can't expect Mrs. Abbrams to spend the rest of her life tending our kid."

"Where'd you go on your honeymoon, Hev?" Howie asked. He wished he had kept the question to himself. It was an intrusion, something nobody did, not into Heviathan's personal affairs.

"Still waiting on that happy occasion, brother." The chastisement in Hev's voice was quickly gone. "But me and Marlys are kind of thinking about a vacation to Tybee Island one of these days."

"That day is today. Let's go," said Howie.

"You idjit. Tybee's a good four hundred miles away, clear south of Savannah. We can't--"

"We got us a car."

"You mean I got us a car."

"We got us two good women."

"Right about that."

"And I've got me four hundred dollars burning a hole in my pocket. That's a dollar a mile. We can do it, dollar a mile."

The four fell silent. Each looked at the other and finally stopped with eyes focused on Howie. Four hundred dollars was a lot of money, especially for a fellow just turned twenty who worked on the looms for ten dollars a week.

"You don't believe me?" said Howie. He pulled the wad of money from his left front pocket and placed it in Hev's hand.

"So that's what that was," Indella said. "I thought it was. . ." She caught herself before she got any further with such an embarrassing admission. But nobody was paying her any attention anyway. Four hundred dollars had them all preoccupied.

"Where did you get so much--" Hev asked.

"I saved it."

"You gotta earn it before you can save it."

"That ain't counterfeit, is it?" asked Marlys. She had never seen so much money in her life. She was not sure if there was that much money in the world, much less in the possession of her newly pronounced brother-in-law.

"We played a lot of poker in the C's," Howie said. "And I was lucky, I guess."

"Four hundred dollars is a hell of a lot of luck!" said Hev.

"Watch what you say, Hubby," Marlys said, rubbing her abdomen.

"Like I said, luckiest son of a broom maker this side of New Orleans. So, what say? Tybee Island?"

"Oh, let's," said Indella.

After a moment of reflection, Hev shrugged his shoulders and said, "Hell, brother, it's your money! You wanna spend it, I ain't stopping you."

3

They honeymooned in Jasper instead. It was Indella who insisted. "Four hundred dollars is a lifetime of living," she said, and Howie knew she was right. Besides, she had a grandmother who lived in Jasper, Carlotta Burkett whose second husband, Curtis Mayes, preached at the Mount Olive Primitive Baptist Church in nearby Elijay.

Nobody had a good time at all, staying with Granny Burkett and having to listen to Pastor Mayes' preaching dawn to dusk. Especially Hev. One night of honeymooning and he was ready to head home and see his baby.

Once they were home, Indella demanded that Howie use part of his poker earnings from his days in the C's to locate their own place. "Get me out of my mother's house!" she said with heartfelt sincerity. What he found was a two-room efficiency apartment above Slaughter's Drug Store on one of Douglasville's side streets. She loved it. The tiny little place became her home overnight.

Once settled with all the amenities they needed for keeping house, Howie set out to find better work. He hated the loom. It had enslaved his papa, his Momma, and was in the process of enslaving him if he did not take matters into his own hands. Hev had escaped it well enough, getting a job at the local soda pop company, driving the delivery truck. That was why he could afford a third hand Chevrolet coupe: the pay at the Coke Company was good. Marlys, of course, hated that her husband was involved with that evil beverage, Coca-Cola. Everybody knew it was filled with sin and shame and led unsuspecting youth to involvement with more serious forms of dope. The feeling against the fizzing liquid was so strong that the area of town where the bottling factory was built became known as Dopeville. And even though part of Hev's pay was in the form of free soft drinks, Marlys refused to imbibe. Hev did. And she accused him of some day going down the same path that is traversed by all drug addicts.

Of course, the manager of the Coca-Cola Company bottling factory turned Howie away; he had no openings at the moment and did not expect any. Try again next month. And so on.

Next he approached the butcher on Main Street. No experience. Sorry. From there it was to the grocer who just laughed at Howie's suggestion that he be given work; some joke. Then to the court house where he asked to take the civil service exam to join the police force; what did he think he was doing, going there without a high school diploma to prove he knew what he knew when in actuality he didn't know much at all.

It was the same all over. You had to have experience and to get experience you had to have experience. The catch of all catches and there was no way around it.

At the end of the week, he visited with Hank Fishborn who owned and operated a small canteen just outside the gates to the cotton mill. "How you doing?" he said in greeting.

Hank was seventy if he was a day. Not too long ago, he had spent a month regaining his strength after a near fatal heart attack. And before that, he had fallen off a couple of crates, stacked so he could reach the top shelves, and broken his left leg just below the knee. He still hobbled from that accident. So to be asked how he was doing was a private joke that only he found funny. "Not bad for a crippled old man," he said. "What can I get you, bubba, and how's married life?"

"Marriage is everything you've heard about it, Mr. Fishborn."

"Sorry to hear it. What'll you have? A ice-cold beer?"

"What I'll take is the whole shooting match. Outside, inside, I'll buy it all."

After he stopped laughing, Fishborn said, "What're you talking about, son?"

"I heard" (he was lying--he hadn't heard any such thing) "that you're in the market to get rid of your little enterprise. Talk on the streets is that you're nearing retirement and want to pass your business on to an upright and industrious young man. Well, sir, that upright and industrious young man is the one you're looking at."

"Don't say. On whose streets you been hearing such talk?"

"All of them."

"Well, the talk's all garbage. Now, what'll you have, Howie, and no more of your foolishness."

"I'll give you three hundred down plus ten percent of the weekly take for the next five years. That's assuming you agree and sell me the whole shebang, shelves and what's on them, roof and what's under it. And give me a couple months of working for you so I learn the ins and outs. I'll work three months for you for nothing, just groceries for Indella and me and maybe a little cash for a new dress for my dear darling. Ten per cent on gross income should be a sizable chunk of money, Mr. Fishborn. Maybe as much as two hundred dollars a month? Over five years that'd be. . . a lot. A hell of a lot."

Mr. Fishborn looked at Howie as if he was somebody he had not seen before. What had happened to the shy second son of May Lou and Alexander Stevens Cobb? "Where'd you learn to talk like this?"

"Spent a year in the C's, sir. You learn a lot in the C's."

Hank Fishborn placed a cold bottle of Coke on the counter and said, "Enjoy while I tend to my customers. But don't leave, bubba, we've got to talk."

That night, Howie announced to his unsuspecting bride that she was sharing a home with the proud new owner of Fishborn's Canteen. "We shook on it," he said. "I'm renaming it: 'Della's Place.'"

And she hugged him and hugged him and led him to the bed where Howie's success story came to an end.

4

Okay.

You're desperate. It's been three months and you can't seem to, well, you know. There's a major part of being married that requires that you. . . Hell, why did God put such barriers in your way and make it so damn difficult for you to talk about certain things? Things like. . . Ah, come on, Howie, it's not that difficult to say "Fuck!"

You hate that word. It's not what you and Indella do, anyway. You make love. That is, you try to make love. Damn. Must be something terribly wrong with you. You ain't normal, boy, and that's the God's gospel.

You wait for Hev to make his twice-weekly delivery of Coca-Cola to the canteen. And now he's here and you take him aside and you whisper to him, "Can you come by my place tonight? We've got to talk."

"Bout what," he wants to know.

"Just something. Come by, okay?"

"Okay."

So he comes by and you meet him at the door. "You can't come in," you tell him.

"Why not? You asked me over here."

"You just can't. Okay?"

"Okay."

"Okay."

"But I thought you wanted to talk."

"I do," you say. "Only not here."

"Where then?"

"Let's walk down to the Canteen," you say and push him out the door.

"Marlys is gonna want to know what this is all about," he says as he strolls down the long stairway to the street. "She was wondering why you wanted to talk tonight. She's gonna want to know."

"Well, you can't tell her."

"That serious, huh?"

"Damn serious." And you turn down the side street, heading toward the cotton mill and your precious canteen.

"How you like running the pub by yourself, brother?" Hev asks.

"Not a pub. It's a diner. Don't sell anything harder than beer and you know it. Don't sell much of that 'cause nobody wants to drink beer in a canteen. They'd rather go to the pubs. Damn prudes."

"You drink your beer, don't you?"

"No, can't stand the taste. You want one? I'll spot you a beer when we reach the canteen. Okay?"

"Okay."

Indella was home alone, despondent, lonely, growing bitter. Howie had left her again, and she understood why. She would leave too. It was all her fault. All her blankity blank doing and she wanted to cry.

What she wanted was somebody's shoulder to cry on.

Even though it was nearly dark, she walked the three blocks to Hev's and Marlys' little house. She could not have been more pleased when she found that Hev was not home. He had gone calling on Howie. Didn't Indella know that Hev was at her house?

"Oh," Indella said, "I couldn't talk to Hev, especially not about this."

"About what?"

"You know. . ."

"Religion?"

"Lord, no. . ."

"Politics?"

"Heavens, Marlys!"

"Then it must be sex?"

Indella almost protested, but was pleased with herself when she said, "Yes. . . that."

"So, what do you want to talk about?" Hev asks, sipping his beer.
And you say, "You know. . ."
"Religion?"
"For God's sake, Hev."
"Politics?"
"Christ, you're no help."
"Then, sex, right?"
And you almost protest, but say in spite of yourself, "Yeah, that."
"What is there about sex you need to know, little brother?"

"What is there about sex you need to know, Indella? Seems pretty simple to me."
"Well, I've got this problem."

"Don't tell me," Hev says a glint in his eye. "You've got you some on the side. What's her name?"
And you nearly punch him out. "No!" You protest with every ounce of energy in your possession.
"Then what?"

"What sort of problem you got," Marlys asked. She had sympathy in her voice, her sweet, almost sticky voice that Indella dearly despised.
"It's my participation." She took a deep breath. If she couldn't tell Marlys, she couldn't tell anyone and if she couldn't tell anyone she'd never be a proper wife. "All this sex stuff," she whispered even though no one was within a stone's throw of where they sat on the front steps. "All this

sex stuff is so damn important now that we're married, you know?"

"Don't I ever know. Hev nearly wears me out sometimes, I swear."

"Huh?"

"I've got this situation, Hev," you say, face blushing-- you can feel the heat behind your eyes. "It's private, brother, you know?"

"Sure. Private, and it'll stay private."

"Swear?"

"Give me a break, will you?"

"Well," and you swallow deep. This isn't easy. But if you don't tell your brother, who can you tell and if you don't tell anybody, then how are you going to be a fruitful husband? "It's like this. Indella and me've been married over three months."

"I know that. I was there, remember?"

"Well, the problem is, I'm still a virgin." There. You've said it. It's out there for the whole world to see and take pot shots at. God, what have you done to yourself, Howell Madison Cobb?

"Are you sure?" he asks.

"Sure I'm sure. Don't you think I'd know something like that or not?" Jeez. What did you have to do, draw it out for him? Paint him a picture and pencil in captions?

"Well, have you--tried?"

Your brother thinks you're a stupid idjit. "I know how it's done, Hev," you tell him, wishing you'd left well enough alone. After all, it is probably a minor thing that you and Indella can take care of on your own.

"Listen, Howie," Hev is saying, sincerity in his voice and caring in his eyes. "If you know how its done--I mean, if you know where it goes and all that, then why's there a problem?"

And you thought this was going to be easy!

"The situation is"--Indella took a deep breath--"the situation is simple: I'm still a virgin."

"My word," Marlys said. "Ain't you and Howie been married these last three months?"

"Of course, silly."

"Then, what's the problem? Don't he know what he's about?"

"The problem is"--and she blushed even deeper--"My problem is that I'm too tight."

"My problem is"--and you blush worse than you can ever remember--"My problem is that I can't hold it."

"Hold it?"

"I squirt my stuff too soon, Hev, is that so difficult for you to understand?"

"Well, don't get mad at me about it."

"He can't. . . get in," Indella said. Oh, how she wished she had stayed home and not started all this. "Maybe we should get a divorce," she whispered. My goodness, she had actually used the "D" word. She could not believe she had said that.

"Oh, no, no," said Marlys, filled with good humor. "We can do better than that. I have the same problem sometimes, Della. Secret is: buy you some Vaseline."

"What can I do, Hev?"

"Nothing to worry about. I had the same problem."

"Get on with you--"

"Seriously. Marlys helped me through it--"

"You talk about sex with your wife?!"

"Better than talking to Momma. I still have the problem, only I deal with it, nothing to it."

"So what do I do? What?"

"Talk to Marlys!"

You scorn his suggestion until you realize he was only teasing. "I'll explain the process to you," Hev says, "as I walk you back to your place. You're gonna be fine."

"Process?" you say.   Holy Ghost, what have you gotten yourself into now?

5

So.

You do as Hev says.   You take your time in the bathroom, take care of things, and don't come out until you know perfectly well that you're primed and ready to go.

When you come out, you're naked except for the socks on your feet and you have chill bumps running up and down your spine, and you're hard and eager to give it a whirl.

Only Indella has other things on her mind. She's still dressed and has been sitting on the edge of the bed, a brown sack in her hands, waiting to get to the bathroom.

"Where you going," you ask, embarrassed for your obvious readiness for her.

"Won't be a minute," she says and disappears, the lock to the door being slipped into place.

You lie on the bed, your readiness slowly slipping into oblivion.

In a few minutes, the latch is released and Indella steps from the bathroom, leaving the jar of petroleum jelly on the back of the washbasin. She is naked now, more beautiful than she has ever been. She stands there, letting you get your fill of her loveliness. She runs her hands over her full breasts and lets them slide down her belly until they reach the area that most entices you. And you're ready again. Fact is, you've been ready all along. She slips under the covers and waits for you to join her.

And you do. And you're firm. And she is moist. And you do it. Your penis finds its way inside her and meets the barrier you did not know was there and she whispers softly so even you can hardly hear, "Push." And you do, and the barrier gives way and she moans slightly and you don't know if it's from joy or pain, and for some reason you don't care, and you are there, you are in paradise, you are whole. You finally consummate that most sacred of places, the wedding bed. And you're thrilled and relieved and awed and filled with the maximum of love for your wife, and your being alive, and your brilliant brother who knows everything there is to know in this world. And you hold your remarkable wife close, caressing her, telling her you love her with every particle of your being.

"Was it good for you?" you ask, afraid of the answer.

"It'll get better," she says, and you don't have any idea what she's talking about.

6

"Well?" Marlys asked. "How'd it go?"

Indella shrugged. She liked playing her little games. She wanted to keep Marlys in suspense as long as she possibly could, but her joy was too intense. It spilled out of her in a series of girlish giggles. "It wasn't bad," she said.

"Tell me about it," Marlys said, pressing close.

"Marlys!"

"Well?"

"It sort of felt good. Hurt mostly." Indella did not know if she should ask, but then she realized the opportunity might never present itself again. So she blurted out, "Is it supposed to start your monthlies when you do it?"

Marlys grinned and nodded. "You mean the blood."

"There was so much of it."

"Didn't your Momma tell you anything?"

"Sure." She said, "Stay away from men. They'll do you dirt.'"

Marlys cozied closer to her sister-in-law and whispered, "The blood's natural for a virgin. It comes from busting through the hymen. That's the special membrane that virgins have? It gets busted when the male organ shows up. That's the painful part. Next time, it'll be totally different. You wait and see."

"You mean--" Indella took a deep breath and wished she was not so naive. "He'll want to do it again?"

"And how!"

She thought about it, pushing the idea around in her head. Sure, why not? It seemed to give Howie pleasure. It made him more attentive. He had touched her in ways he had not touched her before, and she had enjoyed that most of all. She wanted to tell Marlys about that as well, but felt it was something that belonged between her and Howie. It would be their secret and share it with nobody. And if he decided he wanted to do it again, she'd more than likely say, "Sure, why not?"

"What yawl having for supper tonight?" she asked, pleased to finally get off the touchy topic of sex.

"Fish sticks and Coca Cola cake," Marlys said.

The two women hooked arms and traipsed down the road, talking of food and babies and the strange things that seemed to please their men.

CHAPTER FOUR
Howie Cobb Goes To War

1

You remember noise. A constant clap rattle of thunder all around you. Seemed strange, creating so much artificial thunder. And lightning.

Artificial lightning. Really something. Some early evenings the spectacle was better than the fireworks of a hundred Fourths of July rolled into one. The zigzag of tracers, the sudden midair collision of a small plane with anti-aircraft fire, the electric tracings where deadly fire zoomed looking for something to hit.

Mornings were less noisy. Sometimes. Nights, too. Sometimes. Twilight, though. God. You scan the horizon where the sun is setting for possible Zeros looking for anything that moves. Every day seems like with the sunset, here they'd come. Low over the water. Like sometimes, they'd rise up out of the water. Just all of a sudden, there. Coming in out of the sun. Heavy bombs suckered to their underbellies. Extra fuel tanks on each wing. Low and cunning. Zippers you call them. Nips riding in Zeros equal Zippers. Lunatics every last one of them. Looking for death, not counting their own. Something about "The Divine Wind." True spirit of the samurai, only their swords were propeller driven cans of death. Kamikaze and they were all out to kill not just anybody. They were intent on killing you.

And after a week or so of dodging the sons of bitches, you get just as crazy as them. You see them coming and you hop up on the gun turret and wave your shirt and yell, "Here I am you fucking bastard," and you quack because after all, what are you but sitting ducks. After awhile all your buddies are quacking, too. They see the joke, and the punch line is all of you combined. And after that, after the sun's gone and no more Zippers to worry about, you laugh your self sick by quacking at strange times. Like as you vomit your bowels over the side of the ship and quack like you have no sense left. And maybe you don't. It's hard to tell who's craziest, you or the kamicrazy.

How long can a body take it, day after day, always the same, on the tense side of being awake. Even asleep below deck, it's always with one of your ears expecting the wail of air strike. And come twilight, never fail, you hear the song, "In coming starboard, man the poppers, kamicrazies loose from the nut house again."

Here. Think of it this way. You ever bumped into a honeybee's nest? Then sat back and watched the little buggers swarm around you, looking for something, it didn't matter what, to pop with stingers? The same with the Zippers. The honeybee has one shot at protecting its nest. One pop with its tail. And the stinger, if it finds home, leaves the bee's body and enters yours, killing the bee, and giving you a fiery sting that needs your grandmother's snuff remedy to make it feel better. And if enough of the buggers get you, well, it's possible, been known to happen, they can kill you. That's the idea, I gues,. behind the kamicrazies. Honeybee mentality. Protect the nest. At any cost. Whatever the toll, pay it and protect the nest. Once, over a thousand bees took after a beagle hound named Nancy, the one you'd raised from a pup, and enough of them struck home to kill the poor bitch. Of course, each bee that made its hit was killing itself as well. But that's nature, right? That's the way of things. Protect the nest.

Well, like the kamicrazies coming out of the sun. Their object? To die gloriously and to take an enemy with them. You're the enemy. That's God's gospel.

Like with honeybees, one wasn't usually enough. Half a dozen, maybe, with well-placed hits, could bury a ship. You don't know. It's not your place to know. All you know is you hate the sons of bitches and pray to Jesus your watch is early a.m.

You see what your praying gets you. Ha. It's your watch, see? Twilight. Sun's setting like a deflating yellow balloon. You're hanging over the edge, eyeing the school of fish breaking water around the drop line and wishing you had a pole, a hook, and a bobber. Can't hear a thing. You're in the neighborhood of some of the big mothers, the "Death by Fire" you call the battleships and their row on row of flame spitting peashooters. The New Mexico a couple hundred yards away is putting the crunch on somebody over there on land. For most of the day, the guns have ripped the island apart like there is no more need for it on this earth. Even when the pea shooters take a breather, which they do, usually after sundown, you still can't hear. The ring of cannon fire will be in your ears when you die.

So it's your watch, and you put the clamor from the New Mexico out of your head and concentrate on the sea. Good looking water here, considering, a blue like no other blue in the world. And the sky, the sun's beams trying to slice through the thick haze of the smoke screen your ship has helped lay around the fleet, only the wind's too brisk and the screen is whipped away about as fast as the destroyers put it in place.

For some reason, you look up away from the horizon. Maybe something moved. An albatross or sea gull. You don't know for sure, but you look up and Holy Christ, you nearly shit your pants as you eye what must be twenty of them. Not low and humming just above the tops of the highest waves, but coming down, straight down out of the cloud cover, somehow undetected by radar, untouched and unnoticed. Until you put your whistle in your mouth and blow for all you're worth. The sirens blare through the fleet, sounded boat to boat, one loud monotonous surge of sound that everybody who hears understands. The kamicrazies are back, in full force, and aiming straight for the core of the battlewagon. Which sits like the quacker she is, vulnerable and pristine, a magnet with the power of importance stamped all over her. The fifteen seconds it takes to unlimber her anti-aircraft guns are five too many. The lead bee is home free, a clean shot, and a breath away.

You watch as the single bomb penetrates the New Mexico's foredeck and sends a spray of fire and shattered metal two hundred feet in the air. But the kamicrazy's not done yet. His dive is clean and unhampered. This guy knows what he's doing. You admire him and his samurai sword that out of destiny and sheer luck is aimed clearly for the New Mexico midsection. The rapid fire of anti-aircraft is useless so late in a dive. And you watch as the Zipper disappears into the giant ship's maze of metal and flesh. You watch as smoke and fire silence the big ship's guns. And you remember: you're supposed to muster to your own battle station.

So you man your post as your anti-aircraft pistols start raking the twilight air with a near constant fire. You don't quack this time cause you know, without the mother ship's big guns pecking away at the swarm of bees, you really are nothing more than a God forsaken sitting duck, for real this time.

You're at the turret and you're doing your job and so is everybody else on your team and you're sweating and your sweat plops on the turn base where it sizzles like spit on a wood stove. You're feeding the gun with an endless stream of lethal cones and you're not sure what you're shooting at until your buddy standing at your elbow, his sweat mixing with yours, whimpers a sorrowful sounding "Oh, sweet lord Jesus. . ."

You look where his eyes take you and you see it too. The sun as backstop, the propeller as grid, the Zipper with the kamicrazy at controls has picked you for show and tell. Your motor reaction to feeding the gun continues though your head's not connected to the activity any longer. You glare at the approaching airplane and know this is your time, mother dear, going to meet your maker here in this God forsaken hell.

The gun you feed lowers its muzzle and bellies fire non-stop into the speeding kamicrazy, and he takes it all like a gift, absorbing lead and explosives like a sand trap takes on water. And you know that in a minute, now less, you're among the maggot breeders who have populated this stretch of sea. You dig in your pocket for a photo of your sweetie from back home, Indella, I'm so glad you ain't here, and grasp her image into you tight and warm, readied for the concussion that is coming, coming, zipping straight for the bridge of your nose. . .

The explosion is a spray of water and a burst of flame a hundred yards across the spit. You take a chance to look, and the pilot, the kamicrazy himself, is strapped in his cockpit, surrounded by salt water and sinking metal. His eyes are open and you swear you look inside the man's eternal soul and what you see turns your sweat cold.

"How come you missed?" You want to scream. " You were ready, Goddamn it, and the fucker flat out missed. You sonofabitching stupid idiot, how come?"

Then you see the cockpit explode from inside, sending a shower of glass into the oily water. Through the hole comes a gloved hand holding a revolver which is dropped heavily into the sea, then a shoulder and another gloved hand, and finally a head with slant eyes and yellowish skin. He is coughing and blood is drizzling down his face. He works his way free of the sinking cage of a cockpit and slips easily into the churning sea. And before you know it, your guys are tossing him buoys and lifesavers and lines and you watch as the Nip, just a little cuss, grabs hold and clings to the buoy for dear life.

He is pulled aboard. He makes no struggle. He stands at attention even though it is obvious his left arm is shattered below the elbow. His pants above the left knee have been ripped open, revealing a deep gash along his left thigh. There is blood on his face and shame in his eyes. He is alive and he shouldn't be. The bee that failed to protect the nest. Not worthy to live, to have been born.

A bunch of you gather around. You've not seen a real live Jap before, and you have to admit: he don't look like a whole lot. Not only is he short but he's thin, weighs no more than ninety pounds. Needs some of your Momma's home cooking. And you look in his face and see a kid, a mere child of no more than sixteen, clear skin and jet black eyes. You wonder are you fighting children now? Is that the enemy you've been sent to destroy?

One of the brass comes along and takes the Nip below. He has no fight left in him. He goes, no longer a kamikaze, now just a puny little boy, waiting to be tossed back into the sea or into a cubbyhole somewhere and gazed at like an animal in a cage.

The Zippers are finished for the day. You breathe again and wonder if you'll be quite so ready next time. After all, the sun sets anyway, it doesn't matter if you watch it or not.

2

Your watch is up and you can't wait to get below deck and crash into your bunk. It's been far too long a day and you're ready to leave the war making to other folks.

Your buddy catches you by the sleeve and says, "You wanna see the Nip?" And you say, "What for? Done seen him."

"He's in the forward hold, shaking like an aspen tree."

"How come? You guys scare him?"

"Don't you think you'd be quaking, too, you was a prisoner of war of the Japanese?"

You hadn't thought about it that way. It could happen, you know, in this the strangest war man ever made. You make your way to the forward hold. There's already a crowd of swabbies hanging around, making fun of the little Nip, poking at him with their fingers and talking "JaJa" to him as if they expected him to understand.

The prisoner, his wounds now bandaged and the oil washed off, just sits there, staring at his boots. He doesn't even seem to breathe. "You sure he's alive?" you ask the closest swabbie. And the swabbie says, "Give him a gun and let's find out."

The game of "poke fun of the prisoner" soon wears thin and everybody slips away. But you're intrigued. Except for the slanted eyes and skin tone, the kid could just as easily be your younger brother, Pierson. Same height. Same lack of meat on the bones. It makes you a little homesick, being so close to somebody the age of your kid brother.

Soon it's just you and him. That makes no difference: he still shakes. "I ain't gonna hurt you," you tell him. But he keeps staring at his boots like he's afraid somebody's gonna steal them. "No need to worry about that," you tell him. "Those boots ain't gonna fit nobody else aboard this ship." You laugh. He don't.

In a bit, an orderly shows up with a tray of food straight from the Captain's table. Give him the best. Makes sense to you. How often does a tub like the Circe get to take on a prisoner of war? Treat the bugger like a

*king and maybe the word'll get out and you'll be taking
more prisoners than the Marines.*

*The orderly puts the tray on the floor near the Nip's
uninjured right hand. "Enjoy," he says with a smirk.*

*The prisoner makes no move to eat anything on the
tray. You wonder why. You know it smells damn good to
you and you've already had your mess. Must be something
wrong with his tastebuds, not wanting to eat such delicious
vittles.*

*You stand. Maybe he just wants to be alone awhile.
That makes sense, too. So you lift your right hand, wave it
a little, and leave. "Must be tough," you say as you head
out the door. "Sure enough, must be tough."*

*But you can't get the little fella out of your head.
That look on his face as his plane entered the water, so
close you could almost touch him, was one you know you'll
never forget.*

*It's middle of the night when you get out of your
bunk and make your way back to the forward hold.
Nobody's standing guard. No need to. The Nip is chained
to lead pipe; he's not going anywhere. Since your ship
observes nighttime blackout, you carry your small
flashlight with you just so you don't fall into an open hatch
and break your neck. You shine the beam in the prisoner's
face. His eyes are still open, staring at his boots, but he's
no longer shaking. That's a start.*

*"You doing okay?" you ask as you squat in front of
him. You see the tray of food is still there, untouched.
"Hey, buddy," you say, "you gotta eat." You bite into a
chunk of chicken. It's cold and greasy, but you make a face
like it's delicious and then hold another piece out to him.
He doesn't move.*

*You shrug your shoulders. You've done your best.
And as you stand to leave, he moves. Just his eyes, nothing*

else. His eyes move up and latch onto yours. And you stare at him and him at you. Still, he doesn't touch the food.

"Back when I was a kid," you tell him, "my Daddy's brother, my Uncle Sol Cobb, got out his old twenty two, best rifle ever made and decided he was gonna shoot him a chicken hawk that kept taking his chickens. Well, blame if he didn't do it: ping, took that old chicken hawk right out of the sky. Hev and me--Hev's my brother, short for Heviathan, stupid name--took off after that hawk and found it, wounded but still alive. So we determined we'd make a pet of him, put him in a chicken coop and tried to nurse him back to health. You talk about something beautiful: that chicken hawk was a thing of wonder. We tried everything, but the dang bird refused to eat. Finally, one day, we went out to admire him, and he was dead. Done starved himself to death." You look him deep in the eyes and say, "You ain't that stupid, are you? to starve yourself to death?"

Of course he don't say anything. How could he, him being a foreigner and all and not understanding a word you say to him.

You squat back down and take a piece of Spearmint chewing gum from inside your shirt. It's fresh; you just traded for it that afternoon. You unwrap it and break it in half. One half you put in your mouth and chew, the other you offer to the Nip kid. Low and behold, his right hand makes a move in your direction, reaches out, and takes the half piece of gum and puts it in his mouth. At first there is a look of surprise on his face. Then a slight smile. He nods, and you nod back.

"Damn good gum, ain't it," you say with a huge grin on your face as you offer him a second piece, a whole one this time. He takes it and nods as he puts the second piece of Spearmint in his mouth. Only he doesn't chew. He swallows it whole. "You ain't supposed to--" but by then

it's gone. Well, at least you can rest easy. The little fellow ain't gonna starve himself to death this particular night.

Next morning you wake to the sounds of more kamicrazies. Only this bunch is hitting the fleet closer to the island. You stand on the bridge, watching the fray, thanking Jesus that during the night, your skipper's taken the Circe out of harm's way. There aren't that many crazies this morning and the show is over about the same time as it starts.

You head to the forward hold. You have a few minutes before your watch. You want to say good morning to your new buddy.

Only, he's not there. The hold is empty. What happened? Did he get loose and throw himself in the sea? Or worse, did an angry sailor come during the night and throw him overboard?

A junior officer is standing nearby. He says, "Looking for the Nip?" and you say, "Yes, sir," the way you're supposed to.

"They transferred him to the Toledo early this morning. She's heading to Pearl and figured they could take him along."

"Thank you, sir," you say. Damn and you'd invested in three packs of Spearmint chewing gum. Well, you could enjoy them, and with each piece, you'd think of the little fella from somewhere in Japan, a place you figured you'd never get to see.

3

You don't count the days. One after the other they come. Some you spend picking drowning seamen from grub tubs not lucky enough to attract a kamicrazy with rotten aim. Others you transfer supplies.

You don't count the days. One day the kamicrazies started their show. One day they stop. Must have run out of planes. Or pilots. Maybe both.

The shelling stops, too. One day. The noise, the thunder and lightning, just stop. Not from want of ammunition. Plenty of that, plenty stored beneath your boat's crust. And you see a sight that sends little cold shivers up your spine. It's the good old stars and bars, flapping from atop the highest hill on the island over there.

So that's it. You're done with it. And none too soon. You climb aloft for the first time since Operation Iceberg began and take a look at the world you've been so magnetized by. And you stand agog. The sea is churning with the screws of a thousand ships. Didn't know there were so many boats in the world, much less on your team. Thunder makers, every one. Then you gaze at the landmass that had caused so many skippers to man their rudders into this part of the world. Sure as hell don't look like much. Not anymore.

You can just bet once upon a time the island was a real sight to see. Somebody's paradise. Probably green, probably flowers growing tall and lush. Only now, it's nothing. Stripped clean of anything seeking life. A desert. Like Nevada. You once rode the rods across Nevada, and you stand amazed. The desert you see across the water is man-made. You helped make it. And you get a funny feeling inside your stomach like you're going to lose your lunch. Cause for the first time you think, Sweet Jesus, there were people living over there. They must all be dead. Have to be. The landscape you gaze on is lifeless, and will probably stay that way for God knows how long. Forever maybe?

Word comes that the guys can take a dinghy across the sea if they want and take a closer look at what the might of the fleet has wrought. You shake your head. You don't want to see. Too ugly a thing, this thing called war, to ogle like sightseers combing Myrtle Beach. You opt to sit on your bunk and write letters home and pray that the Lord sees fit to deliver you safe and sound when all the fuss is over. Word is that the next landing, the one just ahead, is going to make the one of the past three months seem like a walk in a park.

That kind of strolling you'd just as soon leave to somebody else.

4

You're in dry dock, getting refitted with bigger guns and better anti-aircraft gear. Word is, Operation Iceberg taught the higher ups some lessons, the fleet losing more ships and manpower during the single engagement than it had lost during the rest of war. Swabs like you, thousands of them, gone to feed squid.

Here's what you hear and it makes you squirm at night. The next assault will be against the enemy mainland where they say a hundred million human souls have vowed to die for their emperor. The kamicrazies were using the last little sortie as a practice session for bigger things yet to come. There are a million floating time bombs in the inlets and bays of the mainland, each controlled by a man sworn to steer the vessel into the bowels of enemy ships. There are new types of explosives they tell you that are the size of Alka Seltzer tablets. That the enemy can carry in his mouth or stuffed up his rectum, and all he has to do is shit it out to blow himself and everybody within ten yards of him into God's presence. Your guess is it takes evil demons to devise such ridiculous ways of killing yourself and other people.

No way, you figure, you want anything to do with the next mass assault. Operation Iceberg was enough. It taught you all you need to know, and what you need now most of all is a free trip home. This next one, they're calling it Operation Butterfly for no reason you can figure, is best left to the next batch of swabbies who've got ideas in their heads that war's a heroic thing. You have a wife back home and two great little kids, the new one you've seen only once. You've got a mother and daddy who reared you, imbibing you with a trust in the Lord, and brothers and sisters, some still in school, others already signed on to help with bringing the Evil Empire to its knees. You have enough reasons to live to say the hell with Operation Butterfly.

Operation Butterfly. Whoever thinks up code names is a sadistic son of a bitch.

So. You're drinking, see. Been drinking since dry dock and liberty. Nothing else to do aboard ship except eat and sleep. Sure, you promised Indella you'd never drink. That was before you learned about the wastefulness of war. Maybe Sylvester knew what he was doing, being drunk all those Saturday nights. Without drink, you can't get your brain to close down.

So you and your buddies do everything but bunk at Rosie O'Grady's and gain fortitude for Operation Butterfly from beer and rot gut. The stuff you pour inside you tastes like kerosene but you drink it anyway. Helps you with staying alive though you're not sure what the stuff is doing to the lining of your innards.

The radio blares sweet music that makes you want to cry. Homesickness, you're the Andrews Sisters crooning love songs like there really is some meaning in this life.

The music stops but you don't pay it any attention. You can barely make out the rhythm from the cannon fire you still hear inside your head though the guns have been silent for a couple of months now and you're starting to wonder if maybe you've got some sort of ear damage that needs tending. On the radio now, you see, is a man talking to you from across the ocean, from an office in a marble vault somewhere in Washington, D.C. And your buddy by your elbow jabs you and says would you listen to that, not heard the man's voice before, and you ask which man's and he says, "You know, the boss, the President." And you say that's not FDR, who you trying to shit, and he says, "You asshole, FDR's dead, that's his pinch hitter, a fellow named Truman."

FDR was dead? Why hadn't you known that? Where in hell have you been, sailor? And you know: you been in hell that's where you've been. And you feel queer inside, like the world's not right, not any more. Since you can remember remembering, FDR's been in charge. And you've come to trust him that his way is--was the right one and more than likely the only one. You sat around the radio back home even before this damn war cranked up and listened to the man chat for hours at a time and you knew he knew what he was talking about. Safe. That's what FDR meant. Being safe. And he's dead? You should have known a thing like that. The world should die, too, if FDR's no longer around to give it hope.

So you look at your buddy and ask him, "When?"

And he looks at you like you're out of your ever-loving mind. And maybe you are. He says, "Will you listen to what the man says, for Christ sake."

Why should you listen? There's nothing listening to anyway. You plunk some money down on Rosie O'Grady's plank of a bar and stagger outside. Surprise. The sun's just at noontime and here you are far from sober. But the news, FDR's dead, sobers you enough for you to know it is hotter than West Texas on this tiny little Pacific atoll, and the air's so thick with the sea you feel like you're *drinking from a well bucket each time you draw a breath. FDR's dead. Why hadn't your daddy written you and told you life as you had known it is over with, finished, kaput.*

Your buddy's by your side again. His sweat makes you want to vomit, but then your sweat is probably just as rank. He slaps you on the shoulder and almost shouts, "THEY DONE IT!"

You wish he'd leave you alone and let you mourn the way your daddy taught you back when you were a kid. You want to go some place and cry your eyeballs out, like you did when your favorite uncle of all, your Uncle Sol on your mother's side, got struck by lightning while reading the Sears Roebuck catalog in the crapper. Since you couldn't cry in public, you had gone to the woodshed and let her rip. But here, you don't know where the woodshed is.

"Are you listening to me?" your buddy insists. He's in your face and won't leave you alone. He holds your shoulders in his hands and says slow and even like he's talking to a lamppost, "They harnessed the power of the sun, so Truman says, and they blasted the nips from here to Hell and back."

You don't know what the hell he's talking about.

"The war's over, you fool blockhead," your buddy says and shakes you like a beanbag. "Read my lips. The war is over. We're going home. . ."

If you'd been bone sober, you wouldn't have cried, would you? You would have kept those tears tied up inside until you found the woodshed, don't you think? But you don't know where the woodshed's at and you're drunk as ten skunks, so the tears go streaming down your face, and you don't really mind because there's tears streaming out of your buddy's eyes, too. You don't know why your buddy's crying, but you, your tears are for FDR. The man who had no call to die and leave the world an unprotected place.

5

Your buddy was right on one count, wrong on another. Right, the war was over. Thank God. Operation Butterfly is stored away in a dark vault you figure, fodder for future folks with nothing better to do with their time than to puzzle over whether the tactical deployment of military forces would have worked or not. Wrong, you're not going home, not for awhile yet. There's still work to be done, the skipper announces, different sort of work, the kind you'd just as soon leave undone or to somebody else, but you don't have much say in such matters.

Here's a job for you. Along with the rest of cargo and transport screws of the Northern Fleet, your tuna boat's given the task of escorting the defeated army, seeing to it that the enemy gets the very thing you want—a trip home. The sorry excuse of an enemy army is strung from Manila to the far reaches of China. Your bunch you pick up some place off the Korean coast, hundreds of them. They got no other way to get home, so for the first time you see them, smell them, and ogle while they ogle back. They're bivouacked in Sibley tents, relics of the other great war, and your charge is to keep them moving up the planks and on toward the rear of the ship. Hundreds of them, just like the one you fished out of the sea, all the same, skinny, short, dour, and ragged. The war has left its mark right in the midst of them and you don't feel a bit sorry. They brought it on themselves, right? If you had any say in the matter, the whole bunch of them would walk home and that'd be an end of it. Then you could go home yourself and hug your wife and get to know your kids. God knows you need hugging, it's been too long.

The Nips come aboard. Who would have believed this, you wonder, Nips taking up space aboard your grub tub, and invited, too. You notice the bivouac of men back on shore appears the same, the group now aboard having made hardly a dent in their number. Other ships'll be along and make their mark. Still, it's the strangeness of the whole thing that picks at you. How long has it been, four months if that long, since you watched the burning hulk of the New Mexico slip into the sea? Or you helped pull charred, mangled bodies of former buddies from the wreckage of the USS Bush? Or you stood by and watched the destroyer go down in less than a minute, taking everybody aboard with her? These Nips are the same guys who were trying to blow every last one of you to smithereens and no bones about it. Now, they were bringing their lice on board your ship. Forget it, you decide. You'll never understand this world.

Four days out and you're making headway for Nipland and you're bunking up top with your buddies. Weather's fine. Cool nights, easy sleeping. The enemy--you got to stop thinking of them as "the enemy," your buddy tells you-- it's your word, you'll use it if you want. The enemy's got free run of the ship, and four days out, some of them are starting to relax. The food may not be much good, but there's plenty of it. The quarters might be a trifle cramped, but they got freedom to move about. You watch them, every move they make. And they watch yours. It's a mutual watching society you've created.

A Nip is standing in front of you. It's dark, but there's enough of a moon to let you know it's really a Nip standing there. He's not much of a soldier, you notice. Much skinnier and he'd float if dropped over board. Short, hardly five feet tall. He leans, too, to his right, like he's not quite on an even keel with the swaying ship. He stands there, not saying anything, just watching you, and you wonder, what in God's name does he want from you.

So you give him your cockiest smirk. He bows low from the waist and smiles back. You don't know what to

*do. Kick him in the teeth? Toss him over board? You take
the easiest route. You bow back. He seems delighted and
bows again, this time twice without stopping. You stand.
You tower over him though you've never thought of yourself
as being what you'd call tall. He bows again and you
laugh. Nothing's funny. It's pathetic. But you laugh
because you don't know what else to do. And he laughs
back, a big robust, insincere laugh that sounds to you like
the guy's been practicing.*

*You figure he wants the place where you're sitting and
you're in no mood to fuss with anybody about it, so you
bow again and start aft. But he stops you. He is holding
out his hands. You stop, you're curious. He cups his hands
and opens them. There in his palm is a piece of blue ribbon
with a round hunk of metal attached. You can tell, the
metal has been rubbed smooth by caring hands.*

"What's that?" you ask.

*He mumbles something in his strange sounding
language and lifts his hands to you. You're not about to
take it, you tell him, not till he tells you what it is. But he
offers it again, holding it close so you can touch it if you
want.*

*You take the metal in your hand. It's heavy, cast iron
or some new ore you've not heard of before. The Nip
struggles with a word that comes out sounding like "Klest."
So you repeat after him, Klest? And he laughs in his robust
way bowing and repeating the word "Hai" over and over.
His gesture is: "You keep it, it's yours, a gift."*

*You figure, what the hell, you don't know what it is,
but your kids might find it curious when you get home. You
fumble in your pockets and find a ball bearing. You had
been playing poker earlier in the day and some idiot had
slipped a ball bearing in the pot you'd won. You like the
way it feels to your fingers when you let them play with its
smooth round shape. You hold it out to the soldier and say,*

"Here you go, little fella, a real honest to God steelie, go play some marbles." The Japanese is delighted with the exchange and disappears into the dark.

Your buddy wants to know what you've got, so you show him, and he says, "Not bad, not bad at all."

You tell him you've got no idea what the thing is, that you'll probably toss it overboard like you wish you could have done the Nip, but he says, "Wouldn't do that if I were you. That's the emperor's official emblem, the chrysanthemum, goes with the Imperial forces wherever they go. It's a good luck charm."

You've got no use for emperors and their official emblems, you say, and your buddy says "Do what you want, but that thing's gonna be worth something one of these days."

You shrug but slip the metal object in your pocket where your fingers find it a pleasant toy to play with. Well, the emperor's crest is just the start. Barter is the way to making a killing, and by the time you reach the island that had been the scene of so much death only five months before and your ship rids itself of its captive load, you are the proud owner of a genuine samurai sword--with sheath-- a Nip bayonet, a live hand grenade, two dozen packs of Japanese cigarettes (which taste like cabbage when you smoke them), and so much other stuff you figure you can open a souvenir shop next to your canteen when you get home.

You don't let on to anybody, but deep inside you, you're almost sorry to see the Nips leave your ship. Not a bad bunch of guys, not really, not when you find you have something in common, a love for trading.

Your grub tub makes three more transport runs to Korea and by the end of it all you own three trunks of barter, plus enough Japanese words to get you the trade you really want.

But the best thing is-- the roar of cannon fire in your head--it's gone. You were working on the Japanese word for "too much" when you were suddenly aware of being able to hear the slosh of the ship making her way through the sea. You almost shouted you were so excited by the return of little noises to your ears. The Japanese man making a trade at the time is so taken by the gleam of joy in your eyes he gives you everything he has and asks nothing in return.

The sound of the sea. Such a wonderful thing to hear.

6

Still, you don't go home. Your kids are growing up and you're not there to be part of it. Your wife sends you a couple of photos but they're blurry and you can't really make out all that much. Her letters to you are sounding more and more desperate. Well, what do you expect? She's just a kid herself, not yet nineteen, with two kids to take care of and a husband half way around the world with no prospects of ever getting home. No wonder you're feeling low these days.

They send you and your screw this time to Qingdao. More soldiers, more transport.

You've never been to China before, so you get yourself a camera, a cheap one, with some of your treasure stored in your trunk. The art of trading was created in China, you discover. These guys know what they're doing. There's no way around them, either. They quote you a price, you counter, they hold firm, you counter a little higher, they hold, you finally make your last move, they hold, and if you really want the thing, you leave. Even if you don't really want it, you still leave, but if you want it, you leave in order to come back. When you do, you make your final offer, and if things hold true to form, they accept, and you've cut *yourself a deal. It's the leaving in order to come back that does it. It takes awhile and a lot of useless stuff from your cache, but you finally get the camera and thirty rolls of film. You figure that most of the rolls have been exposed, but it's the chance you take.*

The Nips you board at Qingdao are more battered than the ones from Korea. These guys come from the Fifth Army you're told. They'd been fighting since God knows when, first against the Chinese, then the Russians, and now they face their first Americans and you can tell, they don't know what to do. From the looks of them, most won't make the journey alive. Not enough flesh left on them to do much good. You could feed them ten meals a day and it wouldn't make much difference. Yeah, you figure, there'll be a hell of a lot of burials at sea this run. And even though they're nothing but Nips and coated with lice and carry diseases you can't name, still, they're human, right? And they're getting to go home, right? Something you can't say about yourself.

All aboard and bedded down, your team weighs anchor and points the bow into the wind. You watch as the China coast slips into the sea and you wonder, will you ever be this way again? You shrug. Who'd want to?

7

Having the Nips around is starting to feel normal. Though all have the freedom to roam the ship, only a few actually take advantage of it. The rest sit on their haunches, glare at the sea, and wait.

Since they don't find their way to you, you visit them. It feels like barter time to you. You saunter with your buddy among the Nips who see you coming and rise to clear a way. Without fail, they bow, some deeper than others, some with nothing more than a careful nod of the head. You bow or nod back. You learn to greet them in their language, and some learn to answer back in yours. It doesn't matter how often it happens, each time one of them chimes in with a big "Good Mornink," or "Tank you velly much," there's this big laugh among them. And the same is true when you struggle with "Kun-eech-ee-woah!" Big laugh then from everyone around.

If you didn't know better, you'd not mind befriending some of these guys. They seem nice enough. Quiet. Actually peaceful. Though their acts of aggression since way before you were born would belie using that word, "peaceful," to describe them. Then again, it's a matter of deciding what to believe and what not, there being so many tall tales of horror and deprivation attributed to these people. Like the rumors of Nanking, you don't know what to believe. Or the death march at Bataan, or the building of that bridge, where was it, Burma? It's hard for you to imagine these men being part of the war that saw so much pain and misery. Or the suicide squads. There had been rumors of whole squadrons of these men back during Operation Iceberg who threw themselves over cliffs to keep from being taken prisoner. Or of blowing themselves up with hand grenades as long as somebody else, somebody like you, was around to go along for the ride. Strange, but seeing them up this close and recognizing that they're just men, like you, it's difficult to see them as the enemy you had been taught to hate for such a long time. Like the little Kamikaze fellow from before: just another human being with likes and dislikes just like you. You wonder, if things were different, if it was you being escorted home by them, if they had won the war, would it change things or not? You have no idea. That's one of those things you'll leave to the scholars who get paid big money to figure such things out.

"You know where we're taking these fellas, don't you?" your buddy asks as the two of you sit on the bulwark with backs to the wind.

*Of course you don't know such a thing. How does
your buddy expect you to know such a thing when all you
are in this man's Navy is a carpenter's mate, for God's
sake?*

*"To that place," your buddy whispers as if he's afraid
he'll attract the attention of some unknown god or
something by talking too loud. "The place," he says,
"where they got bombed to kingdom come."*

*You say, "They got bombed just about everywhere
before it was all over."*

*And he says, "No, the big one, the atomic one,
Hiroshima. That's where we're taking them."*

*Hiroshima. The name. You've heard it used at poker
games and during football matches. It stands for hell on
earth.*

*"That's where these Nips were based," your buddy
continues. "The Fifth Army came into and out of
Hiroshima, and that's where we're taking them back to."*

*"What for," you ask. From what you've heard and
that's not all that much, there's nothing left in Hiroshima.
It was reduced to a desert, so you heard. Fact is, nothing's
supposed to grow there for seventy-five years. That's the
rumor. And it's hard to tell just what it is that'll grow there
even then. No plants. No insects. Nothing, not for seventy-
five years. So it's a logical question you ask: "We're taking
the Nips to Hiroshima? What for?"*

*And your buddy laughs like you told a big joke. But
joking aside, you're serious. These Nips aren't all that bad.
A few are a bit grumpy, but who wouldn't be? They're
friendly and peaceful, at least now the war's over. Why in
God's name would anybody want to go to that place, that
atomized desert, Hiroshima?*

*"You gonna take shore leave when we get there?"
Your buddy wants to know. And you're not sure. After all,
visiting such a place as that, the idea's awful new to you.*

You'll have to think about it a while and see how the chips fall.

You're closing in on reaching the place, you hear. Only a day and a half and you'll see the homeland. Gotta be ready for that with your trusty barter camera. Have it in hand, loaded, waiting. You're determined to capture that first hint of the Nips' home nest that they'd struggled so hard and long to protect. Only thing, the wind's rising and the waves toss the little screw you call home this way and that, huge walls of water, coming at you from every side. And rain. Sheets of rain crossing the bow parallel to the sea.

"Where's this hurricane coming from," you ask your buddy.

And he laughs at you. "Stupid idjit," he says to you with a smile. "Hurricanes are for the Atlantic, not out here. This here's a full fledge, one hundred percent big blow, a typhoon, for pity's sake."

Typhoon. God. You've seen just about everything there is to see. It's time to end this crusade and get back where there's solid earth beneath your feet.

Typhoon. You stand, grasping the railing to the turret with all you've got and marvel at this sudden show of power from Mother Nature. "Ain't this something," your buddy screams in your ear as the grub tub you're aboard starts acting more like a bucking bronco than a naval transport, and you feel like you need to clamp onto the saddle horn with both hands but you don't know where it's located.

"Best get below," your buddy shouts, hardly loud enough to be heard over the wail of wind and aching sea.

But you're not about to turn loose of your hand hold. It's all that's keeping you from sailing overboard and into a sea that for all its beauty seems awful hungry right about now. So you cling for all you're worth and pray the blow will finish itself soon and proper.

The next wave feels like the ship's about ready to call it a day, but somehow, you and your screw come through it fine and dandy. The wind is howling like it's mad at somebody. The rain hits your back and head like its made of b.b. pellets. A real humdinger of a typhoon. Wait till you tell your wife back home about this. Oh how puny your little grub tub feels right now as it's blown this way and that, taken like a kite in an updraft then dropped into an angry trough of boiling sea. You wonder, will the higher ups be able to keep the tiny vessel afloat.

Your buddy's gone below to be tossed around like potatoes in a stew pot. Your head tells you you'd been wise to have gone below with him, but now it's too late. It's cling for dear life and hurry with wrapping your belt around your wrist and lashing it to the rail. So what if your pants fall and your butt is revealed in all its whiteness to the rest of the crew. At least you'll be on board when the storm gets finished with its spiteful fit.

Then you see him, the skinny, shoulder-sloping Nip, standing midship near the side rail, not holding onto a blessed thing, just standing there, like a statue. Or a man in prayer to a being greater than himself. And you know, the crash of the waves across the yard's enough to sweep the deck clean of everything that's not fastened down or lashed to a hold. If you know this, surely the Nip knows it as well. Yet there he stands arms slightly raised, hands together at mid chest, head slightly bowed. He claps twice and raises his head to the wind.

And you holler out, "Best get down below where you belong," only you figure he can't hear you, and even if he could, he wouldn't understand.

But then, maybe he does hear you. He turns in your direction, gives a little bow like he knows you've been there all along and what's ahead for him, and you bow back. Habit. Or could it be respect? Does it matter?

By sweet Jesus, he's coming over. It's all you can do to keep your footing and you have something to hold on to plus a belt lashing you to the ship, but there he is, strolling across the deck toward you as if he was out for a walk on the beach. He reaches your rail just as the next big drencher from the ocean crashes across the bow.

Your right hand automatically grabs a handful of the Nip's uniform, and he clasps your arm tightly, a grasp that speaks of a strong desire to live. Thank God for the belt holding true, otherwise the two of you would be but faint memories, with asterisks by your names stating both parties lost at sea.

Once footing is again secure, you stand there, thankful to have survived yet another drenching. The Nip drops his grasp and you feel blood rush back into your wrist and fingers. He bows again, this time more deeply and with a sense of thanksgiving. And you bow back, just as deep, just as thankful. "Pretty lousy weather," you say, You don't know why you say such a thing. You say it for yourself, you decide, more so than for him.

You start with amazement when the Nip replies, "When you live in Japan, you become accustomed to such weather as this." Good clear English. Better English than your own. He obviously senses your bewilderment because he says, "I learned your language during my high school studies and perfected it by taking a degree from the University of California, Berkeley."

"Be Goddamn," you whisper.

"My dream was to remain in America and write Japanese poetry in English," he says, "but the war began, and well as you American's say, 'the shit hit the fan' along with my ambitions. And now where are we, do you know?"

You shake your head, No, you don't know.

"We are a few hundred miles from the Japanese homeland. A place to which I have no intentions of returning."   He is silent for a moment before he asks, "What part of America are you from?"

You tell him and then advise he grab hold as another wave inundates the ship. He grabs hold of your offered arm and you feel the pulse of life surging inside him.

When the two of you have righted yourselves and found air to breathe rather than salt water, he says, "My home was Hiroshima."

You nod. You understand his use of the past tense.

"I have not heard from my family there since the bomb."   He sighs a sigh like none you have ever experienced. Then he says, "You have children?"

Again you nod. You say, "Two boys."

And he grins. "Two girls," he says. "And a beautiful wife."

"You, too, you tell him. Most beautiful wife in the world. Can't wait to see her again."

He is silent for a long time, bracing himself for the crashing sea. Then he says in hardly more than a whisper, "If I had the proper utensils, I could do this with more dignity. But with surrender, there can be no dignity left." Then he takes a small leather bag from inside his tunic and places it in your hand. "May I entrust this to you?"

"What is it," you ask.

"My burial bag," he says.   "In it are my remains along with the address of my wife and family who live-- lived--live in the village of Ushita, north of Hiroshima-shi. Would you perhaps deliver my remains for me to my wife, if she is still alive? The address is written in Japanese inside."

Well, Christ, you want to say, who does he think he is? You're a carpenter's mate, nothing more, not a delivery boy or a messenger from the telegraph office. You don't know this man from a broke windlass and he knows you even less, so why make such a request and at a time like this?! You are bathed again in the cold unruly sea. As you both spew water from your mouths and noses, you look in his eyes and he looks in yours. You have no idea what he sees, but in him you see a dead man. He is a husband and father just like you, a son to somebody, a grandson to somebody else. Just like you. "Take it yourself," you say.

"If only I could," he replies and places the small leather bag in your hand.

You don't know why you take it, but you do. You look at it with question marks in your eyes. "Don't concern yourself with the language," he says, reading your mind. "Show the written message to anyone in Hiroshima, and they will guide you to my wife. I should say, they will guide you to where my wife lived before. . . If no one is there, please scatter the contents on the ground and leave. Is this too much to ask?"

You almost say Damn right it is, but you slip the bag inside your rain slicker as a crashing wave, one of the largest yet, floods the deck with frigid sea. You can't be sure what you'll do, keep the bag, drop it over the edge of the ship once you're alone, or what. But it's there, safe for the moment and the man nods his recognition of his fate, now cradled by the bosom of this stranger, a former enemy, probably enemy still.

"Thank you," he says and bows.

"You better get back below," you tell him, "or lash yourself to the ship. One or the other," you say.

He bows again and strolls to the center of the deck. Not aware it seems of the challenging sea. The ship is creaking from the strain the sea is causing it. The wind has increased in intensity, and there he goes, strolling with no protection back to his original place in the center of the deck. And you wonder, what utensils he was referring to before. Maybe he didn't hear you and your warning to get down below. He stands there, facing into the wind, head slightly raised, his hands clasped in front of him in prayer, prey for the next hungry wave that you know is bound to come. The next will be the biggest yet, sure thing. Always are.

Then he glances your way, his black eyes slicing away at you and you make eye contact with him one last time. This is a man you could come to like, maybe even trust. You wish he would come back and join you, let you lash him to the rail, protect him from the dangers of the sea. But then you understand: this is what he wants. Death a million times over rather than the disgrace of surrender, submission to capture and prison. Confrontation of loved ones, having fallen below the level these people have grown to adore.

You've heard tales of such things, that the samurai spirit which lives in each and every one of these people will not permit surrender. It's not an option. That's why there weren't as many of these guys waiting for transport home as you might have expected. Rumors were all over the place regarding certain Nip units still in the jungles of Asia holding out for the next war to begin, starving themselves, so you hear, just because they refuse to count themselves among the captured.

A samurai does not submit to being a prisoner. He'll chose death anytime.

And you carry his burial bag tucked safely inside your slicker though what you're going to do with it you have no idea. You stand there, lashed securely to the rail by the belt of your pants, watching a samurai face into the raging storm, an English speaking samurai, American educated, better educated than you, waiting for the very thing you know is bound to come--a gigantic slashing wall of water that will send you and most of your ship inside the sea for a baptism and when you emerge on the wall's other side, the deck will have indeed been swept clean of everything not fastened down.

The wall comes. You watch as long as you can manage it, hoping to see the praying Nip grab the nearest spar or dash for the closest port, but he doesn't move. The wall is not as big as some that have washed across your bow, but it is big enough. You are baptized yet again, soaked through with briny water that tastes like salt tea. You gasp as you come free of the wave, pulling delicious sea air into your lungs and checking the loop of your lashing to make sure it is holding as it should.

Then you check for him. The deck is swept clean, just as you knew it would be. . .

Jesus Christ, you've seen a lot of things since joining this man's Navy, but the work of that stupid Nip is a first. And you know, no matter what, if given the same choice, you'd never choose what that man did. You'd always choose life. No matter what. Jesus, you want to shout at somebody, it's not right, this godforsaken tradition of hara-kiri. What kind of religious fanaticism is this anyway?! You want to scream--you've got a wife and two kids at home waiting for you to return! How dare you do this to those who love you!

You may not have bought all the religion your Momma had slammed down on your head all during your upbringing, but enough of it has stuck so that you know there is an all powerful God out there looking after every last living creature on earth. It makes no difference what size you are, or the color of your outer layer, or the way you eat your food or breathe your air or figure your rent-- you're all creatures of a loving God and savior. Don't these people know that?

You wonder if the samurai had been praying to the same God. Or is there another one, the God of the Suicide, *a god that demands glorious death over the insult of capture, a god that he, the Nip now gone, erased for eternity, fish food, found too compelling to avoid? You don't know. You don't want to know. And the look in the Nip's eyes when the two of you had somehow or other connected will probably stay with you the rest of your life when the fact is, you'd just as soon forget it, sooner the better.*

You won't.

As you ride out the typhoon from your point of safety, feeling the surge of nature all about you and the power of the All Powerful, you talk to your lovely wife whom you barely know and your Momma whom you know all too well and tell them both of your deep abiding love, not only for them, but for the Grace of God they both had sorely wanted to share with you. If only they could hear your words, it would ease both their minds knowing that after years of resistance, you accepted Christ's blessings while lashed to the deck of a Naval transport ship in the middle of a sea that just claimed the life of another human being.

You lean with your body into the rail. You close your eyes. You don't care to see any more, not this night. And you wait for the storm to either claim you all or quit its trying.

8

Your bunk is the only thing on the ship you can say is yours. Six feet long, two feet wide, four feet deep, valuables stored under your pillow. Nail the top in place and you're ready for the undertaker's words.

The air you breathe is used. All of it, used. You wish you could lay claim to some fresh air when you lie down at night, but there's none out there to breathe. Not between watches. Not when you want to sleep.

*It's not just the air either. You take a whiff and know
why the human animal has survived. Not its intelligence,
though sometimes when you look around you you wonder
how the word ever got added to the list of human traits.
You take a whiff and realize it's the human aromas that
protect it from extinction. Human skunks.*

*Only, skunks can control their aromas. Whereas
human beings? Forget it.*

*Sometimes you wonder why the skunk has gotten such
a bad rap for itself. You've encountered many a skunk in
the woods, one even getting you personally, full throttle, yet
even that one can't match the rancid aromas emitted by the
human male. In close quarters. Multiplied by hundreds.*

*Stale air. The mixed aromas of unwashed feet, bodies,
heads, and mouths. So many farts there's no need to count
them. Upchucks in corners. Sweat. Wet clothes and dirty
bedding. Sores that refuse to heal, runny with white pus
and crusty with red scabs. Toilets left unflushed. Waste
baskets with chicken bones left from meals five days before.
Nothing like the human animal to build its protection out of
stench.*

*Stale air. It grows like ticks on hairy dogs. Especially
during big blows like the one just finished. Storms mean
the ports are closed and battened. The air is so thick after
the storm's passed that you can almost see it when you cup
it with your hand. So thick you can taste it with your
tongue. No matter how long you're down in the hole, you
don't get accustomed to it. It hangs on for the duration.*

*Then, once the danger of shipping sea swells through
open ports is past, the air that flows among the bunks is
like manna and you're in heaven. At least, sailing in that
direction. And sleep comes easy then. The best sleeping is
that that follows the typhoon. You sit in praise of the open
ports and snore like a hound dog after a rabbit chase,
peaceful, and God awful loud.*

Until the even louder racket from up top shakes you from the sweet dreams of home. The voice from the crow's nest calls out a message that is passed along from tip to toe, each repeat of the song a little more lively than the one before. Land ho. The homeland has been sighted. Peel your eyes for the sight of a lifetime, the song seems to be saying, because there she is, the land of mystery, shrouded in legend, and shivers of fear and excitement and reverence course up and down your spine as you slip from your bunk of joyful sleep and hustle up top with the rest of the guys for a gander at the prize few of you ever dreamed you'd live to see.

Japan.

She sits like a mirage, black and mysterious, off the starboard bow, and the grub tub is steering straight for the nearest spit of land.

You snap picture after picture with your bartered camera. The black horizon slowly turns dark green as you now make out the shapes of forested hills and mountains that seem to emerge out of the sea like strange Greek gods looking for a tasty boat to eat.

The shiver of goose flesh won't leave you alone. Japan. There it is, bigger than life, the string of islands that for some unknown reason decided to wage war against the rest of the world, the islands supposedly inhabited by a hundred million people ready to die for their emperor. This, of course, before the emperor said that surrender was an okay thing.

Photo after photo. You wonder if they'll come out. Besides, the islands are still so far away all they look like are chunks of rock in a churning sea. The entire crew is on deck along with the human cargo. The Nips gape at the sight of Japan and you wonder how they feel now that the homeland has finally been reached. Could they be joyful being so close to home? Sorrowful since they're returning conquered instead of conqueror? Fearful that their families might not have survived the bombings? Hopeful now that peace surrounds them? Hard to tell. The looks on their faces are the same as when they stepped aboard. Blank. Nothing there but empty stares.

But for the land being in the West, you figure what you're seeing isn't much different than the approach to California. How you wish that were the case. You know how you'd feel, getting home. First thing you're gonna do is reacquaint yourself with your two kids, and then you're gonna greet your beautiful wife in a manner befitting a woman who has waited for you so terribly long. And then, well you'll take it one step at a time. But maybe, if you're lucky, you'll find that special opportunity that will let you provide for your growing family in a fruitful way, some way to enhance your canteen and make it a thing of worth.

God. Who would have thought the sight of Japan would make you think of home. Fact is, you're farther from home at this exact moment than you've been since you left. You wish you hadn't thought such a thing.

So you put your growing homesickness aside by rolling the word, Japan, around with your tongue, enjoying the shape it takes knowing that you, part of the conquering force, are about to drop your rock in the harbor of the enemy. You wonder if maybe somehow there might be a mistake, that the land you see isn't Japan at all but some sort of ruse concocted by the higher ups to play a little joke on all the underlings. But the Nips are too transfixed by what they see for the land to be anything else.

Japan. Wait until you tell the kids about this.

9

The anchor drops while you sleep. Well into the night you had watched the alien coastline shimmer past. You watched until boredom pushed you to your bunk. The islands of the Inland Sea after a while had become much the same. Not much different from being in the open sea, which you remember was also exciting at first. So when you wake and find the boat sitting still in the water, you rush to topside where your buddies already stand watching as another dinghy filled with Jap ex-soldiers shoves itself away from the side of the ship, joining hundreds of similar dinghies from hundreds of other ships, some like yours, others sporting different flags from around the world. Now this is really something, you whisper to your buddy and snap his picture with the flat side of a British warship as backdrop.

Then you let your eyes follow the rows of departing Nips. First thing you notice is the mountain. You take a picture of it. The sharp point seems to dominate the entire island and where the dinghies are heading is straight toward a small port, twenty or so houses, nothing more. The houses have tile roofs mostly, a few thatch, that seem to rise at the corners like tri-corn hats. Already a whole bunch of boat loads of Nips have stepped ashore and the dinghies are making return trips back toward you and your armada of big boats. The ex-soldiers who had been your cargo are lined up in front of the houses and being marched out of sight, to where you have no idea, but you guess "home" is somewhere ahead for them all. And you envy them the joy of putting foot on firm earth. It won't be long before they're all ashore and you'll bid farewell to this place called Japan. Your envy is large enough to encompass every last one of the lucky soldiers. How you wish it was you, reaching home.

"Look, over that way," your buddy says.

And you look. You can barely make out in the early morning mist the makings of another port, a bigger one,

one that's most likely attached to a city. "Want to go there," *you tell your buddy.* "Want to see that."

You give him your camera and lean against the rail. He takes your picture. The sharp pointed mountain behind you should be all the proof you need to say to your kids back home, Yep, you were there.

But your buddy is more intrigued by the far port, the one the early morning fog seems to want to hide. "You should take a picture of that," *he tells you and you ask why.* "Cause that place there is the most famous place in the world," *he says,* "and will be for a long time to come."

"You mean, that's it?" *you ask. The low hanging morning cloud has shown you a hundred or more small boats moored in the bay around what appears to be the top masts of a sunken ship or two.*

"Hiroshima," *your buddy whispers. It's like he's afraid of the word or something and it seems to stick in his throat.*

"Hiroshima," *you answer back and remember the packet of stuff in your foot locker down below.* "This is the place," *you say, and acknowledge your promise made in the midst of the storm. You say to your buddy,* "Let's get a boat and go see."

He gives you that look, the one of you-must-be-crazy or something. But you let him see that you're not, that you mean it, you want to go see.

And he nods. He wants to see, too.

10

With so many grub tubs in the area, all divesting their cargo, getting ashore to the mainland isn't so easy as you'd think. You and your buddy manage a dinghy to the little island with the tall pointed mountain at one end three days after the last Nip is ashore and all the officers have had their fill of shore time. And you explore it, Lord do you explore it! "Ninoshima." You enjoy saying the name over and over in your head. "Ninoshima, little Fuji." It has a song in it, something that's worth setting to music. Only you don't know how, so you simply have it roll around in your head, touching it with your insides and letting it grow like flowers in a meadow. "Ninoshima." It feels good to say.

And visit. The row of houses along the pier are old and drafty. You can tell they're made of mostly wood and paper. You've heard of the firestorms in such places as Tokyo and just south of this place in Kure and you can understand a little, having visited Ninoshima, how such things can happen. Fire traps, that's what the Nips call home. You wonder if they've ever heard of asbestos siding? A siding salesman in this country would make a mint and you log the information away for future consideration.

You wander the narrow unpaved streets—there are not that many in the puny little village. You and your buddy part ways. He's more interested in hanging around the dock, making bargains with the Nips who come from nowhere with their little carts of stuff, hidden beneath tarps and brought out only when no one "official" is looking. You've had your fill of the barter system--here it's called the "black market." No need to mess with it here. Yet your buddy can't get enough of the "challenge" as he calls it. Challenge. You know, these people have been without stuff so long, they'd give you their wives, their cart, their tarp, and maybe their daughter, too, for a single candy bar. "Where's the challenge?" you want to know. Still, your buddy takes it all in and loves every minute of it.

One of the little narrow streets takes you up a hillside and you trudge along, enjoying the feel of solid earth beneath your shoes. The street is now nothing more than a cow path, but you're drawn on, up the hill, on to whatever might be on the other side. Assuming there is another side.

You wander through the village and find yourself in the woods, deep, dark, smelly woods. Like back home. You look up into the filtered sky, shielded by layers and layers of leaves, sometimes a hundred or more feet thick above the path. You are aware of the sounds of deep woods. Crickets, tree frogs, cicadas. Homesickness overwhelms you. You feel the need to cry out, to find your wife, hold her tightly, kiss her and feel yourself grow and explode deep inside her. . . Where have you been, you want to ask the cicadas and tree frogs? God, how you've missed them, and never realized the missing before. You turn in circles under the shade of the trees and remember those days so far removed when you and your wife had finally discovered what it means to love deeply and firmly and eternally. That moment lost like a trinket in a whirlpool. "The Wildcat Den" as you called it. What had it really been like. If you could only remember. But it denies you.

"Yo!" you shout into the woods.

How long, you wonder, would it take to get home from where you stand? Every thing you hold dear, your wife and kids and brothers and sisters and mother and daddy, is half a world away. Yet so close. So very close you could almost touch them. You close your eyes and breathe deep and you are aware of the power of air to propel you through time and space to where you wish you could be. The air touches you in ways nothing has touched you before. The texture, the mixture of water, the perfect smell it carries, and you are no longer where you are. It feels good, so incredibly good you wish you could stand still and breathe forever. But the path goes up the hill. The path goes somewhere, you don't know where. Does it matter? You wander on, knowing that when you reach the crest of the hill, you'll look down into the valley of your home. Maybe. Your loved ones will be waiting for you, open arms, and eager to hold you close. . . It's a dream worth dreaming.

You run. You've lost your running legs from so long at sea, but still you run the best you can. The hill is steeper than you first thought, and before long you are puffing like your Momma's wood burning stove when it's been filled with green wood. Out of shape you admit. You stop and lean into your knees, pulling the water-laden air into your lungs and feeling your sweat pour from your pores, soaking your navy blues. But you don't care. Over the hill, there is home.

Five steps away from the magic of the crest, you stop. No, it won't be there. Home is a million miles away. This is stupid you tell yourself, rushing like this toward disappointment. You're missing everybody far too much. Can't let yourself do that. Can't let your disappointments creep up on you like that. So you forge ahead. It doesn't matter what's on the other side of the hill. It will be Japan. Just another side of an island.

From the top, the cow path continues on, winding down the far side of the hill toward another grouping of buildings, mostly farm houses flanked by dry, weed-infested rice paddies and sheds falling to ruin. The twisting path leads on, and you must follow it. You don't know why; it is simply there to be followed.

An awe overwhelms you. Now that the misplaced sense of home is behind you, you see the world a bit differently. You are alone, traipsing down a foot path in a country that less than two months before was the homeland of your most feared and hated enemy. How could such a thing be? How was it possible to do such a thing? Traipse along like a tourist on vacation. You don't even have a side arm. You're in uniform, yet you're not a soldier. You're not ready to protect yourself if hostilities are still in the former enemy's minds. How could you wander off like this with no protection, with no hint of what might lie before you? Has being at sea so long made you stupid or what? A bend of the path draws you on. There, not twenty feet away, is a totem pole with its carvings painted in bright reds, blues, yellows, and whites. Topping the pole is a winged image, a demon with yellow teeth and red eyes, glaring at you with a viciousness that makes you eager to turn tail and run. But you don't run. You'd seen such a construction several years before when you'd visited an Indian reservation up in the mountains. You'd not understood the totem pole then, you don't understand it now. Yet the connection between your homeland and this, the homeland of the sworn enemy, isn't as distant as you had been led to think. Strange. Of all you'd expect to see on the other side of the hill, a totem pole would be last on the list, if it made the list at all.

Then you see them, the ex-soldiers. Digging. Long, shallow trenches, six feet wide, piling the moved earth on each side of the ditches. As a group digs at one end, another is dragging bundles and dumping them lengthwise at the other. Only, they're not simply bundles. They are--

"My God," you gasp loud enough to draw a couple of diggers' attention.

Where could so many bodies have come from? There is a mound of human remains, stacked randomly on top of each other, and when one body is removed, others slip down the slope of the little hill. The workers wear squares of gauze over their noses and mouths and soon the aroma reaches you and you wish for a square of gauze yourself. Further on, a trench has been filled with hundreds of bodies and you watch as another ex-soldier douses the human remains with some sort of liquid and after emptying his five gallon tank, lights a match and drops it into the trench. The heat from the flame brings new sweat to your forehead and chest and legs, and the smell makes you want to throw up. But you don't. There are places for such shows of weakness, and you know, this is not one of them.

You turn tail. You run. The woods back down the hill aren't like home at all. They are alien. They are threatening and you rush with sweat drenching your navy blues and turning them black. It doesn't matter. How hard you run won't clear your head of the stench of death.

Your buddy greets you at the pier. He carries bundles of black market and you push past him. "Got a ride to the mainland," he tells you, but you're not interested. Maybe tomorrow. Then again, maybe not.

"But the ride's leaving now," he yells at you. But honest to God, you're just not interested.

How far is it to home you wonder, and how long will it take to get you there?

11

You stay aboard. You can't get the smell of burning human flesh out of your nose and mouth and skin.

Your buddy manages a boat to the mainland. You tell him have a good trip.

The Nip's burial bag has shifted to the bottom of your trunk, but you find it and sit on your bunk, staring at it. The man had said, take the bag to his wife. Why you? Why not one of his own kind, someone who spoke his language and understood his customs? The ship had had hundreds of Japanese to choose from for what seems to be an important task. So, why you? You have no answer.

You untie the strings holding the burial bag closed, then tie them back again. Are you curious enough? Do you really want to know? You sit with the bag for what must be an hour before you retie the strings and realize, you don't want to know at all. What would you put in your own burial bag? The picture of your wife and two kids she'd sent you in her last letter. Her last letter, yes, that'd have to be included. The unprocessed film you've taken with your barter camera, and probably the camera as well, plus what little money you had from your last pay. But what else? What sorts of personal things should it contain? A letter from you to your mother, another to your wife, maybe a brief note to each of your brothers and sisters, daddy, and the uncles you like best. But what would you say and how would you say it? Might as well give it a whirl.

You sit the rest of the afternoon writing notes to your loved ones, last notes, a will of sorts, though you don't really have all that much to divest. Besides, what's yours is your wife's too, and your kids. She knows that and will take care of things as they should be taken care of. Dear Momma, you write, but you can't find the words to follow, words that would mean anything and be worthy of a burial bag.

You trace the Japanese writing on the outside of the man's burial bag with your finger. What a lucky bunch of people these Japanese are, you think, to have such a beautiful written language to say things in. And then, the thought comes clear in your head. Though you hadn't really promised anything, still, you have a responsibility. It might have been thrust into your hands without your wanting or desiring it, but there it was, proof of your commitment to a man's last wish. And you feel confused. What are you going to do with this man's bag?

A boat is leaving your ship for Ninoshima. You are on it. You agree to help with the small dinghy's cargo in return for passage to the mainland.

It is midday. And hot. Your shirt is off and pants rolled as crates of food and water are stacked on the Ninoshima pier. "For the locals, this food?" you ask the yeoman in charge of the detail. "Like hell," he says back.

"For the brass. They're setting up some sort of camp on the mainland," he says.

"How do you get to be part of the brass?" you ask, and the yeoman finds your question the best joke he's heard in two years.

You stack the crates on a bigger boat, more crates than you can count. Then you volunteer to go along for the unloading on the mainland. The lieutenant j.g. grins at this sudden surge of volunteer help. He understands, everybody on board wants to go to Hiroshima and gawk. "Number one tourist attraction in the world," he says. You don't say anything. Let him think what he likes.

12

The train from the port is carried on new tracks. Where you get on is a mess. No signs of bombs or anything like that. Just a mess. Too many people living in too small an area with too few places to sleep, not enough food, and nothing to do with trash except let it drop. The people you see are mostly men. In fact when you look more closely, they are all men, most dressed in the tattered uniforms of the military, most with shaven heads and unshaven chins. All move aside when you approach. All bow. There is nothing for it but to bow back. Which you do when you think about it.

They don't ask for your ticket. You're in the uniform of the victor, not haggard at all, so you must be using the train on official business. The conductor, a small man with wrinkled face and dressed in tan loose fitting trousers and shirt, no shoes, merely bows to you as he makes his rounds, asking for tickets from everyone Japanese. There aren't that many on the train.

"Will this train take you to Ushita," you ask the conductor. You have no idea how you remember the fellow

on the ship telling you the place where his wife lived--or lives--but you do. You surprise yourself.

The conductor grins and bows deeper than ever. You bow back and show him the burial bag with its Japanese markings. You assume the lettering forms some sort of indication as to what to do. But you've never really trusted assumptions all that much. The conductor reads the message, nods this time, and indicates with a sweep of his hand that yes, this train will serve.

You thank him in your language and he grins, bowing once again. You realize you're on your own. You wish your buddy was with you but he'd just be in the way, too interested in the black market to appreciate such a quest as the one that drives you on. You smile inside at the thought of "a quest," like some famous knight, you can't remember his name, looking for some famous item or other. You can't remember that either. Or that fellow with his ship, the Argo, looking for what was it, a golden something or other. "God, got to improve my memory," you say aloud.

The Japanese man sitting across from you moves.

Your buddy would never believe this. An impossible "quest."

The train sweeps around the city. You see a hill separating you from the main town; it is green in most places, burnt brown in a few. Tree covered and inviting. When the train stops at a station near the hill, you decide to take a few minutes and go explore, so you leave the train and the conductor bows more deeply than ever.

No one needs to tell you what's on the other side of the hill. Unlike yesterday when the path drew you on toward home, this hike today through the woods and up the steep incline is an invitation to a horror you don't know if you are ready for or not. You brace yourself. You've heard all the talk--one bomb, single instant and the entire city evaporated, turned to steam and ash and melted flesh. But all the talk really means little. It can't be as bad as everybody says. After all, one bomb can only do so much, and though they had given this one a special name, "A-bomb," you can't credit it with the kind of destruction everyone seems to think it created. What lies on the other side of the wooded hill will tell you everything you need to know, put all those doomsday speakers to shame once and for all. But then, what if they're right--can't be. Just can't be. Climb the hill and find out.

You climb the hill and find where the fire had burned itself out. You stand there, transfixed. You don't know what you should be looking at, but what you see leaves you silenced and awed. You sit on a charred stump of a tree, staring across an open field of ash that stretches for miles in a hundred and eighty degree arc. You don't know what to feel, so you feel nothing. Simply sit and stare and develop an ache deep inside your chest that will not go away. Not until you're dead. This you know for a fact.

You are looking at the manifest power of the sun, the ability of man to conquer the unconquerable, to manage the unmanageable, and you are more than awed. You are urged to learn more, to become part of it, somehow, in some way. To know such things, to be able to accomplish such a feat, requires one's most profound awe.

13

You become comfortable, if comfortable is the right word, with Hiroshima. At least you accept it for what it is: the result of the most atrocious as well as the most audacious act against human kind in the history of the world. This is your perception; thankfully, no one asks you to share your feelings. Otherwise you might make the wrong comment to the wrong person. Silence is the characteristic of the city that you are close to adopting as a second home.

You manage to volunteer for numerous tasks that take you to the city as often as possible. After completing tasks at the port, you wander, usually toward the devastation and beyond. Some days, your buddies go with you, but for the most part, your explorations are accomplished alone and generally in silence. Each time you enter the bomb plain, you do so with a moment of prayer and a determination to experience the place fully. Besides, you have your quest. As hard as you look, you cannot find this place called Ushita.

Some aboard your rig try to warn you: it isn't all that safe to wander through Hiroshima the way you do. They mention something about a latent killer left by the atomic bomb, something that is colorless, odorless, tasteless, something called radiation. But you don't care about that. You are involved in your quest.

You also know it is against the law, so to speak, to take photographs of what you experience during your wanderings through the destroyed city. You have been told by more than one junior officer that you should leave your bartered camera on board ship, but there is simply too much to be seen and remembered to take such advice. You have also been told not to wander beyond the postings identifying the range of the atomic blast, but like with your camera, you listen and go about your business as usual. You know what you must do.

One morning your wanderings carry you to where the river splits in two. You have heard of the famous "T-bridge" that had formed a perfect target for the B-29 bombardier, only T-bridge in the world so you think, and there it is, still intact, though buckled pretty bad. You know that at last you have found the so-called hypocenter, the place where the bomb had actually exploded some five *hundred feet or so above your head. It had been here and for quite some distance in every direction that people, how many you have no idea, had suddenly, instantaneously ceased to exist, evaporated, snap your finger and you're gone, that sort of thing. You walk with guarded steps onto the bridge, which seems sturdy enough and find the "T" where another bridge joined the first. You stop, look around at the enormous destruction and snap your finger. That quick. Probably quicker. If you had been standing where you are now on the morning of August 6, less than two months ago, you would have vanished without a trace. You would have felt nothing, most likely. You would have died without ever knowing it. You snap your finger again and think how lucky the person who had been standing where you stand now on that incredible morning was. Remarkable luck. He--or she--had died without ever having to know what had happened to the city he--or she-- called home. Instantaneous death. What happens to the soul, you wonder. Does it evaporate, too?*

You look into the clear early autumn sky. No planes this morning, none with a singular cargo. You close your eyes and lean against the warm concrete of the bridge. You try to feel the souls of those who had died so immediately, but you can only hear and feel silence. "This," you say aloud, breaking the silence for a moment, "is monstrous."

You aim the tiny camera at the ruined building on the bank of the river. Once it must have been quite the place to visit. The central dome must have been magnificent. Now all that is left are the steal girders that are twisted and gnarled. It is one of the few buildings here at the hypocenter that has been left standing. The rest is total ruin.

"Hey, buddy!" The voice slices through you sending shivers of dread up and down your backbone. "What the hell do you think you're doing?"

"Sir!" you say as the MP takes the bridge two strides at a time to reach your side.

"You got a permit to take pictures of this place?" the MP demands.

"No, sir," you say.

"Don't you know there's a prohibition against photographs anywhere within the atomic field?" The MP waits, expecting a lie.

"Yes, sir," you say, standing at attention, ready to salute.

"God. You swabbies are all crazy fuckers." The MP holds out his hand. "Gimme it."

You place the small camera, the one you had bartered for while on shore in Qingdao, in the MP's mitt, regretting that you hadn't been more careful before deciding to take a snapshot of the destroyed building.

"You got any more film than what's in here?" the MP asks.

You know it is time to lie, so you say, "No, sir!"

"Like hell. Raise your arms, you stupid son of a bitch." The MP runs his hands up and down your sides and legs and then searches your rucksack, taking from it the burial bag, which contains the already exposed film from previous trips into the atomic field. "Okay," the MP explodes. "What the hell's this!"

"Burial bag," you say, not needing to lie about it. Before the MP, who seems to be growing more and more perturbed the longer he stands in the sun, could pull the strings apart, you blurt, "Friend of mine asked me to return his remains to his wife. She lives in a place called Ushita. I've not found her yet."

"Friend of yours? What are you, some sort of Nip spy?"

"No, sir! I'm just a stupid son of a bitching swabbie like you say. A crazy fucker and all that. The fellow who

gave me his bag was washed overboard during a typhoon at sea, and he asked me to deliver this to his wife, assuming she's still alive. Sir."

The MP does not open the bag. Instead he shoves it into your chest and says, "Ushita's to the north. Follow the river on the east shore till you come to the place where it splits apart again. Cross the river to the north and you'll be in Ushita."

"Thank you, sir," you say, stuffing the burial bag inside your rucksack.

"I'm no damn officer," the MP says, "so cut the 'sir' shit."

You start toward the east bank of the river when the MP yells, "Hey, Fucker!"

You stop, turn.

"Smile!" the MP says and snaps your picture with the bartered camera. The MP laughs in a sardonic way as he tosses the offending camera over the bridge railing into the river below.

14

Ushita. You are among houses not touched by the A-bomb test, not directly. Houses, more like shanties, some painted white, most with thatch roofs and paper walls, crowd on top of each other, stacked like cordwood. Kids stare at you as you walk like a creature from Mars down the mud streets. Hills covered with jungle like forests rise steeply and the houses rise with them, clinging to the slant with leach holds. You don't know how they get the shacks to stay put, but somehow, these Nips make such housing work.

Here, there is a rice paddy, dry, dead, a deposit now for unburned refuse. There, a flower garden with rose bushes in full bloom and evergreen trees trimmed in perfect shapes. Over there, is a row or two of vegetables, fruit still months away from making it to somebody's table. There a stone Torii rising out of the ground with a trail marked by colorful flags winding through a bamboo forest. Here a stone wall higher than your head, and above it another wall, and another. Here is a graveyard with spires of granite so close they nearly touch. Like the houses, stacked. There, a cat gnawing at a rotten orange left as some sort of token on a row of tiny Buddha's. A strange world you are in. Strange indeed. Here, out of sight of the rest of the former city, you might imagine Japan as it might once have been, untouched by bombs of any sort, poor but surviving. And the people you meet on the streets, part of the promised hundred million kamicrazies, a promise these people seem to have forgotten. For here, now, though dressed in the enemy's uniform, a uniform of war, you are not the enemy at all. There are other enemies now, and you're not among them.

Nobody you meet knows your language. Some turn backs on you and your sailor's outfit. You wish you had other clothes to wear, clothes that wouldn't put these people off. You aren't going to hurt them, you want to tell them. You want to be their friend. Their buddy. Some of the kids come up to you with open palms and you give them what few things you have--chunks of chocolate, sticks of gum, a tin of Spam. They squeal with delight over the chocolate and stare with wonder at the gum. They are just kids, like kids everywhere else in the world, full of curiosity, and fear, and maybe a little acceptance, you don't really know.

You show the burial bag to the few adults who will give you the time of day. They look at it with curious stares, touch it sometimes, but shake their heads, not knowing or not willing to point you in the direction you need to go. You're about ready to curse the fellow who saddled you with such a thing. Maybe he knew you would find a roadblock in your way. Maybe he understood that he was tossing you head first into a purgatory of hunger and fear, and maybe he was laughing even now from his definition of heaven. Big joke on the gullible American boob. And you almost laugh at the cleverness of it. No wonder he gave you the quest. It was his punishment to you for his having lost the war. And you are fool enough to go along with it, to try and keep trying. Fool. That's the right word for you. Wandering the backside of an A-bombed city like some sort of pilgrim looking for some sort of holy grail. A sitting duck for anything the enemy might want to do to you. But do you have sense enough to give it up? If not, why not? Just dump the bag in the nearest drainage ditch and be done with it. Once and for all.

Then the tiny Japanese woman who doesn't run from you or turn her back on you, takes the bag, fondles it with something like affection, reads the inscription on its outside, and nods. "Hai," she says, followed by a string of words that leaves your head swimming.

You hold up your hand and shake your head and say back to her that you only speak a little Japanese, slow down. Then she points. She jabs the air with a twig-like finger and chatters in her language like a Tommy gun.

You hold two hands in front of you and shake your head.

Then she takes your right arm and tugs you up a steep path, up the side of the hill, up past the cemetery, and close to the jungle-like woods. You don't resist though the climb leaves you gasping for air and soaks your blue tunic with sweat. After two days of futile searching, this is the closest you've come to being given hope of making contact with the end of your search.

She stops, points. And you see the tiny house, whitewashed and clean, the size of your corn crib back home, a child, no more than three, sitting on the low step, drawing circles in the dust with a maple leaf. The woman nods her head and shoves you toward the child and the small but immaculate little house.

The child ignores you. It's like she has seen you a hundred times before, she knows you and accepts you, and she doesn't acknowledge you even when you greet her with good morning in her own language. It's like she doesn't know you are there. You notice the baby skin of her face and it seems shadowless, pale and crumbly. Her hair is brittle and appears to have fallen out in several places creating small bald patches of white skull. You give her a chocolate which she takes, and for a moment, only briefly, you catch a glimpse of her eyes, and they are empty, nothing there. You're not sure, you've not looked into the eyes of blindness before, but you could swear you just did. Even in the heat, you shiver slightly, and you wonder, has your wife told you all you need to know about your new kid, the one that was an infant when you were last at home? Could he be blind, too? God, you want to go home so bad.

You stand on the step, peering inside the cramped shack when a small woman comes to the door. The beauty of her tiny angelic face leaves you with nothing to say. You forget for a split second why you have come to her door. Her straight black hair is pulled into a braid that hangs down the middle of her back. She wears a pair of loose fitting pantaloons and a cotton shirt that falls her to her knees. She can be no more than sixteen, you think, so tiny, so fragile, so young. Except for the slant of her eyes, she is the image of the woman back home who is even now, you are certain, tending to the needs of your kids.

You bow.

She bows back.

You hold the burial bag out. She bows as she takes it.

You bow back.

She reads the inscription, the expressions of surprise and joy and intense sadness cross her face like flickers from butterfly wings, and then folds the canvas into her chest. There are tears forming in her eyes and you want to say but can't that the man who gave you the bag had died the way he had wanted, his choice, that he was taken by the sea and not the enemy, that he was a brave and obviously good man who spoke your language better than you, that he faced the sea and his death without fear. But the ability to say anything is as foreign to you as the idea of standing where you do. So you don't say anything. There is nothing you can say.

You bow.

She bows back.

And you leave. Your quest is finished. You are done.

You return to your ship, your buddies, your ticket home, and you cannot remove the look you had seen in her eyes. The look of, "I don't understand." And the look in the eyes of her child, the look of "I'm not aware of anything to see."

And you don't. Either one.

15

"My dear wife," you write, "I miss you so." You wait a moment or two before you add: "and how are our children? Are they well?" The empty eyes of the child haunt you, keep you from sleep. Cause you to write your wife more often than anytime before. You don't understand the impulse. You don't know the child's name, or that of her mother, both living as best they know how in the world created for them, not by them. It will not leave you, even after writing your fourth letter of the day to family and friends back home. It lingers, the look of emptiness in the child's face.

You fill your pockets with whatever you can find: tins of meat and vegetables, rations of bread, sacks of rice, and as many spuds as you can fit inside your cap. Chocolate too. All children need chocolate now and then. Especially this one. And packs of gum. You are a mobile grocery store when you leave your ship.

"Where you going," your buddy wants to know, looking a little miffed that you're taking so much food with you to shore. You want to tell him but you don't think he'll understand, so you lie: "Barter time," you tell him. "Black market calls."

The little whitewashed shack is easy to find. Simply climb the path to near the jungle's edge and there it is. Empty, or so it seems.

You rap on the door jamb but no one is inside. You pull the curtains aside and lean your head in. There is a smell of soap in the tiny room. Soap and soy sauce. You place the contents of your cap on the floor just inside the door and you empty your pockets next to that. The resulting pile of foodstuffs seems so small, so inconsequential. But it is all you can manage without a duffel bag or go cart. Next time you'll bring more.

The childlike voice behind you startles you and you turn. The frail woman stands there, the child, now with purple splotches on her forehead and tummy, in her arms, the baby's thin arms encircling her neck.

"Ohio," you say wishing you knew more of her language. You think you're saying hello but you can't be sure. Regardless, you bow. She bows back.

She sees the pile of food on her floor. She shakes her head and waves at the food with her free hand.

"For your little girl," you say, and hold out a fist full of chocolates. The baby must smell them. She reaches out, her little hand more a claw, and you unwrap a piece of

chocolate and place it against her mouth. The candy disappears, but the child's expression does not change.

"Go," the woman whispers. "No want no more," she says in broken English.

You back away, but you don't reclaim the pile of food. You brought it for her. And it will be hers, no matter what she says about it. After all, your boat is filled with enough food to feed the entire population of Hiroshima, and why it's not happening, you don't understand. Why more food and water and medicines aren't being shared is beyond you. To reach this little whitewashed house, you must travel through the most horrible poverty you could imagine. Starvation. Death. Fires stoked with the bodies of the newly dead. The aroma of death stronger than any other smell. So bringing so little seems not enough, but it's what you can manage. You'll bring more, medicines next time, you want to say, for your child, for her eyes maybe. You don't know. You are confused.

The woman pushes you aside and enters the small house. You wait for a moment, fully expecting the pile of food to be thrown through the curtained door. But it isn't.

You back away. Watching. Waiting.

Then you turn and leave. You'll be back. Of that you are certain. With more food. Medicine next time. Without fail.

16

Things are different aboard ship. Word spreads that you'll be weighing anchor in a day or two and then heading home, back to Pearl, to be decommissioned, sent home with a pat on the back and a "don't-call-us-we'll-call-you" promise from the higher-ups.

Things are different in another way, too. They are searching swabbies like you as you leave ship. Too much black marketing going on.   Too many swabbies like you getting conked on the head and left face down in the rubble of the nuked city.   Scavenging is to come to a halt, the captain says, and you have to reduce the amount of food you take down the gangplank.   Still, you don't stop.   Every day, you trek to the little whitewashed house, and every day the Japanese woman waves the food aside.   Still, she doesn't reject it outright.   You leave it and next trip it is gone.   Even if she doesn't eat it herself, maybe she is selling it and using the money to get doctors to look at her child.

Today, your duffel bag of food is confiscated on ship and all you manage to exit the ship with are three packs of gum and a packet of soda crackers.   You'll do better, you promise, but today it's the best you can do.   In fact, you're surprised the officer of the watch lets you off the boat in the first place.   With as much food as you had in your duffel, he would have been within his rights to deny you shore leave.   A good-natured sort, he said bring him back some good stuff, and you didn't know what he meant, not exactly.   But you can guess.

The woman seems to be waiting for you when you approach the little shack.   She stands in the doorway and when she sees you, she disappears inside.

You slip off your shoes and follow.   The tatami floor feels cool to the soles of your feet.   This is the first time you have entered the tiny house and you feel you must stoop at the shoulders so not to bump your head against the ceiling.

The woman is not in the small room.   But you hear rustling from behind the sliding paper door.   Which you pull aside.   She stands, her back to the entry, beside a neatly folded pile of quilts and rugs which seems to have been prepared just for you.

She turns.   She has allowed her robe to fall open as she faces you and you see the beauty of her slender body, revealed like a Christmas gift in front of you.   And you're not aware of the fact that you're breathing. She lies on the matting and holds her arms in your direction, but you can't move. It is as if something inside you has gone solid all of a sudden. Except for your wife, you've not known another woman. With her you have made two beautiful children, children you are so proud of. And now, your wife is inside your head, whispering, "It's okay, I don't mind, Go ahead." And you don't understand. How could it be okay? Your mother's voice is louder, almost a scream of repugnance, but you know she doesn't understand any more than you do. Your mother's voice is shouting "Sin, Sin," as loud as it can, while your wife is whispering "It's okay" in her soft and secret way. So you stand, frozen, not knowing what to do, knowing only that the woman lying in invitation is the most beautiful human being you have ever seen.

You have waited too long. She stands, ties the robe at her waist and leaves the room. You sit on the floor in disgust at yourself. What is wrong with you, you wonder, but you have no answers to questions like that.

In a moment, the woman returns. She carries a small bundle as if she is afraid it might break. The bundle is actually a baby's blanket, tied at both ends. She kneels to you, touches your arm with a hand that has the weight of a house fly, then unties one end of the bundle. She pulls the wrapping aside.

In it is the body of the small girl child, and a swell of pain and regret, of disbelief and disgust, emerges from you in the form of hot tears. "Dead," the woman whispers so softly she might as well not have said anything.

And you swallow her in an embrace that you hope will never end.

17

All shore leave is canceled. Orders from the captain himself. Just too much black marketing going on, that and aiding and abetting the enemy. Aiding the nips by stealing food and medicine from the United States Government and giving it to the enemy, building them up, helping them grow strong again, strong and eager to lead the assault against our homes, our way of life. So, to stop it once and for all, shore leave is over. From this point on. Nobody is to leave the ship except on official business, and only then when accompanied by an officer.

But you've got to get ashore, you tell your buddy. Omiya is waiting for you, expects you, needs you. Not to mention what you need. Omiya. Yes, you tell him, you finally learned her name. When you had taken the body of her child to the fires, you had asked her what name to give the baby so you might offer a prayer in her honor to the Lord Jesus. And she had told you, "Noriko." So you had placed the bundle on the wooden pier and slid it into the blaze, whispering a quiet prayer for her, precious Noriko, hoping your Lord Jesus would be willing to accept a prayer offered for one so small, so heathen.

And without being asked, the woman had touched her bosom and said, "Me Omiya," and you had repeated the word over and over, loving the sounds it made inside your head. You had told her your name, then, but it had been too difficult for her to pronounce. Howell is not suited to the Japanese tongue, so she had called you "Him." That was good enough for you. "Omiya." "Him." There was something almost poetic about it, you tell your buddy.

So you see, you tell him, you have to get ashore. It is already midday and she is expecting you. She is waiting for God's sake, and here you are, stuck, no way to get word to her, no way to say good-bye.

You lean over the ship's rail, and your buddy says, "I wouldn't do that if I were you."

"Do what?" you ask.

And he says, "Jump ship. They wouldn't let you back on board."

And you wonder, would you want back on board. And he answers for you, "We're heading home tomorrow. Home, Howie. Think about it: Home."

You haven't thought of home in so may days now. Seems like forever since you were there, among relatives and friends--and wife and kids. Home. The two bedroom apartment above the pawnshop, side street, a few blocks away from Main. Small town with a cotton mill, lost in the deep hills of north Georgia, a hundred miles from anything important. Except family, wife, kids. Most important of all. The boy, your namesake, but you call him Howbo, nobody knows why, the one you helped your wife birth before heading off to war. Born with a full head of black wavy hair, like yours, a huge voice just right for singing or preaching or running for governor some day. Tiny hands that grasped your fingers so tight he cut off the circulation. The kid was waiting for you, along with the one you've seen as an ugly infant but looks bright enough in the photos your wife has sent. Growing. Both of them, growing, without knowledge of their pa. And your wife's letters berating the fact that the little one, little Winston, too, was a boy. Didn't the Good Lord know she wanted a baby girl? Someone like her? Take the leap and you'll see none of them, and already the youngest is a year and a half old. Don't take the leap and never see Omiya again, not say good-bye, not make certain she has enough food to last the week, not know if the paleness coming to her cheeks was the same sickness that had taken her daughter Noriko, not knowing if more of her hair is falling out today, or if the blue and purple splotches appearing on her forehead and soles of her feet were going away or not.

Choose, sucker. Choose.

You turn your back to the rail and fold your arms across your chest. Not knowing, you reason, may be easier than its opposite.

Regardless, you can't keep the pains of caring from ripping away at your insides as you accept the fact of not knowing.

"You gonna be okay?" your buddy asks, and you say without looking at him, without looking at anything at all, "Don't expect I will."

18

The sea is a placebo for forgetting. It is the gateway to home, and that is where you are bound. You can't get there fast enough. Turn the screws up tighter, and beat it home.

You've got two kids there you're eager to get to know. And a wife you're eager to hug. And another kid you're eager to make. And a mother to tease and a daddy to honor and brothers to beat up. So much to do.

So much.

One of the things to do, and of this you are certain, you think, is return to Japan. To Hiroshima. You'll do it, too, one of these days.

Maybe.

CHAPTER FIVE
All The Folks Waiting At Home

1

Indella had lost touch with her husband. She continued to write him daily, putting the letters in envelopes and rushing to the mailbox every day, hoping for some word in return. Any word. Nothing.

She moped around her second floor apartment, a place that Hank Cobb began calling "The Widow's Peak," for some reason.

"Do you know something you're not telling me?" Indella demanded of him.

He merely shrugged and gave her a leering grin, one that made her skin crawl. He kept coming around every afternoon at sunset asking if she had received any news, placing the emphasis on the word "she," implying that someone else had. Hardly a time came for her to take her babies for a stroll that Hank wasn't someplace about, grinning like he ate the rat's cheese and offering to tote Howbo for her if she wanted.

One day on one of these strolls, Indella stopped and turned to Hank and asked him directly, "Hank Cobb, is there something you want from me?"

He had grinned in that leering way of his and said, "Is there anything you want to give me?"

She told him to go home and not come back around, just go home and stay there.

"Let me walk you home first," he said.

Hev came home from Pensacola with a slight limp. "It'll go away after a few years," he assured Marlys. It was wonderful to have her husband home, limp and all. Hev's being around made Indella mope that much more.

The war had been over at least a month, and still nothing from Howie Cobb. "Do you think he might have found somebody else?" she begged of Marlys, about the only friend she had left in the world since she found Hank's attentions not the least bit friendly.

"Where do you suspect he's going to look, being in the Navy like he is?"

"I don't know," Indella said weakly. "A mermaid, maybe?"

"You're the silliest woman I've ever met," Marlys said.

"Well, ships put into ports and swabbies get leave. You any idea how many hula women hang around ship docks, hoping to lure them a man? Hundreds. I saw the movie."

After a bit of laughing about mermaids and hula dancers, Indella said so quiet that Marlys had difficulty hearing her. "They say those Japanese women are truly beautiful."

"Who is it who says such a thing like that!"

"Hank," she said.

Marlys scoffed at anything Hank Cobb laid claim to knowing. "He's chock full of himself, Della, and you know it. Why, there ain't a hair on his head that ain't crooked. Just like everything in his brain, all twisted and gnarled, and shaped around what he wants from life."

"Still. . ."

"Oh, honey," Marlys said, putting a comforting arm around her sister-in-law's shoulder. "Your Howie's fine. He just can't find any paper to write on. You got to stop worrying."

"I sorely wish I could," she whimpered.

She confronted Momma Cobb, but the old woman had heard nothing from him either, not since peace had been declared a month ago.

Something dire had to be wrong, she told Momma Cobb, who simply shook her head and whispered, "If I'd only gotten him baptized before he went off to war."

"You mean," and Indella seemed incredulous, "that Howie's never been baptized?"

"Oh, that boy. He's got more resistance to religion than any human being I've ever known."

Now Indella really had something to be concerned about. If her husband hadn't been baptized, then he was a --. She could not think the word much less give it shape enough to be uttered. If he should die, and that was what war was all about, men dying, then he would go to Hell, no question about it, and she would never see him again, not on earth or after. Suddenly, Momma Cobb was the villain, the person who was making sure Indella would be unhappy for the remainder not only of her life on Earth but throughout all eternity. "How could you do such a thing!" she demanded of Momma Cobb.

"What? What such a thing?"

"You let my husband leave this Village knowing he's not bound for Heaven if anything should. . ."

"We'll take care of the matter when he gets home, Missy," Momma Cobb said, venom in her voice and disdain in her manner.

"What if he don't get home? What if his ship's hit by a torpedo and sunk and Howie's soul goes the other way? What then?"

"It's called 'faith,' little girl," Momma Cobb said. "Oh ye of little faith."

2

Two weeks and it would be Christmas. But what kind of Christmas could Indella celebrate without knowing what had happened to her man? Howbo was talking miles a minute and Winnie-Pooh, hair down to his/her shoulders, was into everything he or she could reach. Which meant nothing in the house was safe.

It was a Friday when the package arrived. It was wrapped in plain brown paper and fastened with string wound several times. It was addressed to Mrs. Howell Madison Cobb and had no return address. She ripped into the paper and out fell a wad of money held together by a rubber band. And under it was a letter which she read quickly and then a second time with care and understanding.

"My Dear Darling Wife, You know I ain't much for writing and all that, but know I miss you. You are in me to stay, you and my kids. I will be home 'fore you know it. Keep this money safe if you can. I miss you, miss you, miss you. Be home soon. All my love, Howell."

Three thousand dollars. Now, where in the world would Howie Cobb have come up with three thousand dollars. "Oh my God," Indella said aloud. "He's robbed a bank."

3

Indella recognized the rat-a-tat at her front screen. It had been the same every afternoon since peace came and Howie had stopped his writing. She snatched the door open and glared into Hank's grinning face.

"What do yawl want, Hank!" she snapped.

"Thought you might like an apple." He held a half-eaten apple in her direction. It was always the same.

Yesterday, it had been a peach with a bruise spot on it. The day before a can of beer--an empty can of beer. This time an apple with three huge chunks bitten out of it. It reminded Indella of that famous scene from her favorite motion picture, only the sex was different, and the heritage. Hank was a far cry from being a queen, even though he was about on par for wickedness. But it seemed appropriate. Indella had always identified with Snow White. She tried to live her life as she envisioned Snow White living hers.

She invoked her sweetest "Snow White" voice and said, "Go home, Hank. You ain't wanted here."

"Being wanted and needed are two different things," he said, slipping half his body through the doorway. At least now she couldn't slam the door on him the way she had the day before.

"Just what do you think I could possibly want from you, Hank Cobb?"

"Maybe a little human attention?"

"Just who is it I'm supposed to be getting this attention from, pray tell?"

"Why, me of course." He grinned his foolish grin and said, "It's a well known fact that every widder woman needs a little servicing now and again."

She slapped his face. Hard. It wasn't until after the sound of the slap faded into the linoleum of the kitchen floor that Indella realized that Snow White would never have slapped anybody, not even the wicked queen. No sooner had the slap left her open palm than she wanted it back. But that wasn't possible. Besides, maybe that was what Hank Cobb needed, a good spanking and sent to his room without any dinner.

His grin was bigger than ever. "That felt good, hon," he said, as he slipped his arm around her waist and pulled her to him. "You smell good," he said, dropping the half-eaten apple to the floor.

"What makes you think I'm a widow, Hank?" she asked, smelling the same smells on him that she had come to associate with her drunken daddy. They made her want to puke. Maybe that wouldn't be such a bad idea, she thought. Throw up on her sorry, good-for-nothing brother-in-law, and send him home to Momma Cobb with some explaining to do.

"Well, for one," he said, "you ain't heard from Howie in a month of Sundays. Seems to me, if he was still interested in you, he'd of been in touch."

"Got a letter from him today," she said, feeling his grip on her lessen.

"You lying to me."

"You wanna read it?"

"You lying through your teeth," he said.

"Let me get it for you, Hank. Show you what you're missing by being such a stupid ass."

He had let her go, confusion coming over his mouth where the grin had been.

She grabbed the letter from the light stand beside the sofa and held it out to him. "Here. Read it. Read what that brother of yours has to say to his precious wife after a month long silence. You want me to read it for you? Since you're too stupid, I'll read it for you." She was pressing him tighter and tighter against the screen door. "My dear darling wife, You know I ain't much for writing and all that, but know I miss you. You are in me to stay, you and my kids..."

Hank was gone. He was halfway down the stairs by the time the screen door slammed shut. "You better believe Howie's hearing about this when he gets home, Hank Cobb!" She yelled after him.

She picked the apple off the floor and dropped it in the garbage can. Then she walked with the grace and dignity of Snow White to her bathroom and began to run a tub of water. She couldn't wait to get the stench of filthy alcohol off her face.

4

The fourth thing Howie Cobb did when he came home from the service (it was late February and he simply showed up one afternoon unannounced) was to take his second son, Winston, now a year and a half old, to the local barber.

The first thing he did was kiss his wife and swing his two kids around and around in circles. The second thing was to pick his wife up and carry her into the bedroom, slamming the door behind him, leaving two screaming kids demanding attention. The third thing he did was to run all the way into the Village to say hello to his Momma and Papa.

Finally, he turned his attention to his children. "What in God's name," he nearly shouted when he saw the condition of his baby boy: still dressed in pink dresses and ribbons in his hair that was red and curly and hung to his shoulders. "What are you trying to do, woman?" he demanded. "Turn this baby into a damn girl?"

"Yes," was Indella's pitiful reply.

"Well, shug, you want a girl so bad, then let's make us a girl."

"Okay," she said, realizing of course that the chances of their success were about fifty fifty.

"Come on, Bubba," he said pulling Winston's thumb from his mouth. "We'll take care of this hair business right now."

"You can't do that, Howie," Indella protested.

"How come?"

"Cause I worked hard getting her hair perfect like that."

"Her hair?" He shook his head in amazement. Who was this person he had taken as his wife? She was a stranger to him, one with peculiar ideas. "I'm sorry, son," he said to Winston. "I should of been here for you, but we'll take care of that."

Howie took his boy to the barbershop with Indella trailing behind, Howbo in hand, crying out to him, "Don't do it, Howie. Please, let me keep my little girl!" Howie plopped the pudgy kid in the chair and said to the barber over the caterwauling coming out of both his sons as well as his wife, "Give my son a crew cut!"

Winston didn't have any idea what was going on. Some strange man had rushed into his room where he had been playing with his pet June bug, the one with the string tied to its leg, picked him off the floor, and lugged him down the street to a place that stank of cologne. He screamed like his skin was being ripped away when all that was being cut was his long, curly red hair.

Indella finally hushed her bawling. She watched as the tresses flew to the floor. She was not ashamed, either, not in the least. But she knew she was losing her daughter after so many pleasure-filled days. And that made tiny tears of sorrow slip out of her eyes. She wept in silence as the clippers made paths across Sandra Ellen's/Winnie-Pooh's head.

"Oh, Sandra Ellen," she whimpered, picking one of the curls from the floor and slipping it into her apron pocket.

"His name's Winston," Howie insisted.

"I know it," Indella said, wiping the tears from her face and fingering the lock of curly red hair.

To the day of her death, my mother kept that lock of hair safely stored away in a place where nobody would find it. And I've hated barbershops ever since.

CHAPTER SIX
Peace And Prosperity Don't Mean Much

1

My first memories are more fleeting than I want them to be. Damn things. Wouldn't it be wonderful to be able to recall those things that have had such an effect on you? Like that first visit I made to a barber's chair: I don't remember it at all, yet I had been there, or at least somebody with my name and with the same gene pool. All I recall of the event are the intense feelings of dread and sometimes fear.

Memories are fickle. They flit past with little warning that they are even in the vicinity and then they are gone before you have time to take proper note of them.

The strangest things prompt memory: an aroma of warm milk, the texture of the air touching your pores on a perfect day, the sound of a car radio as the auto whirls by. And they, these memories, don't hang around, not for long. You need a portable tape recorder to take note of them before they've slipped back into the recesses of your memory.

Several years back at a family reunion, I overheard my least favorite uncle, Horatio, my Dad's youngest brother, whispering to a tike no more than six: "Better watch out, Buddy," he said. "Tonight when you go to bed, I'm gonna come into ya room and cut your ears off. Feed 'em to my hogs. Better lock your door, Buddy, cause I'm coming for your ears."

Memories rushed through me as I overheard Uncle Horatio that Sunday afternoon. For as long as I could remember, I had slept with some sort of covers over my ears. I didn't know why. Compulsive behavior, more than likely. But as I listened to Horatio's words that morning, I had chills up and down my spine. I can't be sure that he had said the same thing to me when I had been too young to do anything about it, but for the first time in my life I understood why I slept with my ears covered. Covered ears had been the only way I know to protect my ears from being fed to Uncle Horatio's hogs.

I don't know if I remember this or not. I could have picked up on the image from things my Mother might have told me. But then it may be the best kind of memory: those purely remembered. Here it is: I am sitting under a small tree. I am in a diaper. And it is soiled both because of my lack of bowel control and by the cloth being wet and attracting dirt to its bottom. The tree offers no shade. It's not big enough for that. Like me, it is just a young'un. I am singing. I don't think I am big enough to know what a tune is but I'm sure I must have known what it meant to sing. After all, I am sitting under a tree, feeding tiny birds. And they are singing, too, more than likely, so I oblige them and sing back. This is my first memory. The first memory I have of being alive on this earth and it is of singing under a tiny tree feeding even tinier birds. Then the memory's gone. There's no point to it. Nothing special happened. I am simply there, doing my silly little thing. Probably wondering when that smelly diaper was going to be changed. I wish I could pull from this, my first clear memory, a meaningful metaphor for growing up, but life doesn't work that way. Regardless, I've sung all my life, more when I was young than in my waning years, and I've had an abiding love of nature: trees, birds, those sorts of things. Is that metaphor enough?

2

Granny Bea lived at the top of the hill. The little asbestos-shingled house was at the end of the road and she would be babysitter when Indella and Howell were away. Which both kids minded. Glory Bea didn't treat us like we wanted to be treated. I must have been spoiled. But if so, it wasn't my fault. Mother must have developed some sort of guilt complex after the way she treated me in the first week of my life. Her disowning me the way she did caused her to give me far more attention than I needed. But I didn't reject it: I didn't know how. In fact, I abused her because of her guilt, which made me something of a monster. I was a demanding child or so I've been told on numerous occasions by more than one. Most reports today indicate that I refused to eat anything but tomato soup and I was still nursing from a bottle after my fifth birthday. It's no wonder I turned out the way I did, according to Howbo, given my beginning. I make no excuses. I am who I am and expect everybody else to deal with it.

Being spoiled is an interesting way to phrase what I was. I think of what it means to drink "spoiled" milk--the taste is awful and stays in the mouth for hours, sometimes days. Or to be around "spoiled" eggs--the aroma hurts and you can't wait to get away from it. So to be "spoiled" as a young'un is a pretty distasteful thing. But spoiled I was, like it or not.

So, back to what started this diatribe: I didn't like to be babysat by Granny Bea because I was what she called "spoiled rotten." I demanded Mother when she wasn't around and made everybody's life miserable until she came back. Poor Granny Bea. She's dead now. I think of her often. I wish I could apologize to her for the way I treated her. She died of cancer in 1977 and I didn't attend her funeral.

This is my memory. It was a weekend. And Howie had come home that Friday afternoon driving a brand new 1949 Pontiac sedan. It was a sleek looking thing: pale green with ribbed seats front and back. There was a statue on the hood, a woman with her arms stretched behind her and her torso disappearing into the chrome of the hood. The back sloped down in one continuous line from the window to the rear bumper. What a car. I fell in love with it immediately. But I never got to ride in it.

One of the reasons Howie came home with a new car, aside from the fact that his investment in a local grocery store was paying off, was that Uncle Rudolph, a man I'd never met but had heard so much about, was finally back home or at least in the Veterans Hospital in Atlanta, recovering from something or other. I didn't learn what until years later when Uncle Rudy would bend my ears about his problems with alcohol.

Anyway, Howie came home with the new Pontiac and announced that it was time to drive to Atlanta to visit Uncle Rudy. At the time, Rudy's wife, Elaine, and her brand new baby girl, Dena, were staying with Granny Bea. And it was decided that Elaine would accompany Howie and Indella on the trip into the big city of Atlanta along with my new born sister, Trudy, not quite three weeks old at the time. And Dena, Howbo and I were to stay home with Granny Bea.

I was distraught. So was Howbo. Neither of us had had a chance to ride in the new car and here the best of all possible chances, a trip into Atlanta, and both of us had to stay home with Granny and be treated like babies all day long. It wasn't fair. And I let everyone know of my displeasure. I pouted all day long. And I shouted at the top of my five year-old lungs that I didn't want to ride in that mean old car anyway, that it was big and ugly and dirty and anything else I could think of. Granny Bea told me, "When your Daddy gets home he's going to do something bad to you, Winston, behaving like this," like take his belt to me or something like that. And I said, sassing like I'd never sassed before, that I didn't care if he ever came back at all, that he could just be gone and stay gone for all I care, and she gave up on her threats and left me to holler my head off.

Then sometime around mid-afternoon, something strange happened. I had a feeling, a strange, uncommon feeling. I've told my Mother about it, and she termed it "a premonition." This feeling was so strong, so real, so terrifying that I had to tell somebody. I couldn't find Howbo and tiny Dena wouldn't have understood. So I sought out Granny Bea.

I don't remember what she was doing, so I'll make something up. She was mopping the kitchen floor with a large rag mop that was dirtier than the floor would ever be. I stood at the entry to the linoleum-covered room and waited until Granny Bea noticed me. When she finally did, she didn't stop her swipes at the floor with her filthy mop. "Don't you come in here, Winnie Pooh, floor's wet."

"Something's wrong with Momma," I announced.

She didn't stop her mopping.

"My Momma's hurting," I said to her, not really understanding the words.

"You don't know what you're talking about. Your Momma's not even home and you know it."

I said I knew deep inside me that she was hurting.

"That right? Hurting how?"

I said, "Her eye."

"And how would you know a thing like that?

And I said: "I can feel it. My eye. I can feel it in my eye. This one."

And sure enough, my left eye was watering like I had a speck in it. Only I didn't. There wasn't anything in my eye to cause pain. Still, it was throbbing like something had sliced into it and cut away parts I needed to see with.

"I don't have time for your foolish games," Granny said and shooed me back outside. So, I sat the rest of the afternoon on the back steps of Granny Bea's house, rubbing my left eye and trying to get it to stop hurting so much. Only it didn't. It hurt worse.

Sometime later that afternoon, a police car drove up to the front of Granny Bea's house and a man who was dressed like a cowboy knocked on the front door. I sneaked around the side of the house and stood in the boxwoods rimming the front porch and tried to listen to what was going on. I could see that Granny was upset about something. Finally the cowboy went back to his automobile and sat while the engine idled and Granny Bea went out back calling for me and Howbo and Dena to come in.

I approached the cowboy. He looked mean with his huge full-brimmed hat and his arched eye brows and the big pistol strapped to his waist. "My Momma's been in a accident," I said.

"Now how would you know a thing like that, son?" the man asked.

"I know. I can feel it. Is she dead?"

"Now, son--"

I started to cry, hurting eye and all. And he sat there, staring at me, not knowing what to do. I wept because I knew that my Momma was dead. I was certain of that. The feeling I had was too strong. My Aunt Elaine, too, more than likely. I knew that that new Pontiac was a mean and ugly car. I knew it was going to do my family significant harm. (Later I found out the opposite was true. That mean and ugly car had saved everyone's lives. Only I was too young at the time to understand such things.)

Granny Bea had baby Dena in her right arm and Howbo's hand in her left. He was gawking at the officer sitting in his car like he'd never seen a police car before. Maybe he hadn't. "What did you tell this boy, Shurf?" she demanded to know, referring to my tears.

"Nothing," the man protested. "He's the one doing the telling."

"My Momma's got a hurt eye," I said again. "It hurts something terrible. My eye, too, hurts something terrible."

"You think you can drive me over to my sister Azzie's house? She can look after the kids for me."

"Hate Aunt Azzie!" yelped Howbo. "She pinches too hard."

I got in the police car, Howbo and me in the back seat. If it hadn't been for my hurt eye and all the feelings of fear and pain, that ride would have been the best of my life. But I couldn't appreciate it. These God awful feelings were piling up inside me much too heavy for me to appreciate anything at that moment.

Aunt Azzie even had a freshly baked coconut cake, but I couldn't appreciate that either. "My Momma's hurt real bad," I kept telling Aunt Azzie and anybody else who would listen.

The only person who listened to me was Howbo. We sat on the edge of the porch at Azzie's house, whispering. I told him all I was feeling. For the first time, I was able to say it aloud: Momma's been in a car accident and she's hurt real bad. Howie, too. And new born sister. And Aunt Elaine. And there was somebody else, I didn't know who, who wasn't hurt at all. And Trudy had died but been reborn. And on and on. I made up most of it. Only it felt like the truth at the time. Little did I know that most of it was the truth. Sort of.

Howie, Momma, Aunt Elaine, and Trudy had visited Uncle Rudy in the hospital which was somewhere between Marietta and Atlanta. Uncle Rudy's "wounds" from the war were no where near healed at the time and he was afraid he might lose his left leg. So there was little for anybody to do except visit and try to console. After as much visiting as they could take, all had piled into the new Pontiac sedan, which I had called a mean and ugly car and started home.

Howie was a good driver, something to be thankful for. The route they took back to Douglasville was the Powder Springs Road, which crossed Sweetwater Creek somewhere south of Powder Springs. The bridge across the Creek was one-lane. It was long and curved at both ends. I crossed that bridge many times until it was replaced, and it always made me apprehensive knowing that if oncoming traffic didn't stop before entering the bridge something traumatic would happen. On this particular day, Howie pulled to a stop at his end of the bridge and waited for an oncoming car to clear before he started across. He was in the middle of the bridge, moving at a snail's pace, when he saw the delivery truck enter the other end. The driver of the truck hadn't stopped, hadn't even slowed. The truck hit the wood slating of the bridge with the sound of a shotgun going off inside a steel drum. Howie stopped the Pontiac and rammed it into reverse. He was moving backward away from the oncoming truck when the larger vehicle slammed into them, throwing the soft green Pontiac through the rail and to the creek bed below. I have heard rumors that the truck driver never saw the Pontiac, that he was so tired from weeks of hauling stuff from state to state that he was all but asleep at the wheel. What shook him from his near sleep was the sound the truck made as it crushed the smaller car. The truck could not stop until it had cleared the bridge and rammed into the bank on the far side of the road.

Indella had seen the truck coming. She doesn't remember doing it, but she grasped Trudy so tightly in her arms that she crushed the tiny baby. Trudy would have died if Howie hadn't pulled her loose from Indella's incredible grasp and blown air into her lungs. As it was,

Trudy's body was covered with bruises that reminded everyone of her mother's near fatal grasp.

Aunt Elaine in the back seat was thrown from the car. This was in partial reaction to seeing the truck bearing down on them. She opened the back door trying to escape and was thrown clear. The water in Sweetwater Creek saved her from serious hurt. Howie had used the steering wheel to brace against the impact of the truck. It was the whiplash he received by flying off the bridge that caused him the greatest pain.

Indella was the one who suffered most. A piece of the front windshield slashed across her left eye, leaving glass embedded inside her socket. She suffered a broken collarbone and some severe stresses to her arms from Howie prying Trudy from them. There was no way to get the bleeding from her eye to stop. She was rushed to Marietta and the hospital. They did some corrective surgery, sewed her up as best they could, but leaving shards of glass in her eye that had to be removed in subsequent surgery. Also they botched the initial repairs, sewing up her lacerated eyelid in such a way that several of her eye lashes grew into her eye. Indella suffered serious pain in her left eye for the rest of her life.

The truck driver left the scene of the accident as Howie was wresting Trudy from Indella's death grasp. What the truck driver saw was a dead child, a dead three-week old baby, being given mouth-to-mouth by a frantic father. And he had walked away, leaving his truck behind. He blew his head off with a twelve gauge shotgun three weeks after the accident. If only he had remained at the site he would have known that Trudy not only survived but is today the mother of three, living comfortably in the North Georgia mountains.

How do I explain my premonition regarding the accident? I can't. I've had a few other premonitions since, what I call lucky guesses.   Precious little good that particular one did anybody.

3

Aunt Martha and Uncle Beau had a son my age named Grady. I hated Grady. Not because I didn't like him. I liked him a good deal, more than was justified. I hated him because every time I was around him, he got both of us into trouble. I had more whippings as a result of things Grady got me into than for all other causes put together.

Aunt Martha and Uncle Beau lived on the other side of Douglasville, so Grady and I didn't spend all that much time together. When we did, though, we made up for lost time. Grady was looking for trouble non-stop. And he had little trouble finding it.

Once, I got a whipping for going wading with him in the creek behind his house. I was wearing my Sunday best shoes. Another time, I got stuck in a tree that I had climbed out of a dare, and when Howie had to crawl up the tree to fetch me, well, it seems justified, the switching I got. Still another time when Grady and I went calling on his neighbor's kids and they weren't home, I thought it would be okay since Grady said it was if I borrowed the neighbor's bike. Only it wasn't okay. The neighbor kid was obviously fed up with Grady's laying claim to everything around him and again I got a whipping. Not a bad one, to be honest, since I'd done only one thing wrong: trusted Grady. But Howie whipped me anyway, mainly for show.

One time, Grady not only got me a solid switching with a hickory I had to cut for myself, he also got me on Howie's bad side. I couldn't stand that, being on his bad side. So I blamed Grady. It was probably just as much my fault as his, but I blamed him anyway.

Behind Grady's house was a shed that had a padlock as big as a fist on its only door. Grady told of all the wonderful things his Daddy, Uncle Beau, had stored in that mysterious shed. He'd never seen them, of course, but he knew they were wonderful. They had to be. Otherwise, why have them locked away? So one Sunday afternoon when Indella and Howie dropped me off at Aunt Martha's and Uncle Beau's, Grady whispered, "I can get us in the shed."

"How?"

"Come on."

I was six and planning to start school at the end of that summer. So, I was curious. It was the only way to learn things when you were six. I wanted to find out for myself what was so important that Uncle Beau felt justified in using a pad lock.

What Grady had done was dig a hole at the back of the shed. He had already dug under the rear wall and all that was left to do was dig a little more and push our way through the floor on the inside. I was the guest so I did most of the digging and pushing. After all, Grady said, he'd already done the hard work, getting the hole started. It was only fair that I finish it and be first inside the mystery shed.

It took most of the afternoon, digging that hole. The dirt around Douglasville is red clay, and in August it can bake as hard as a pottery bowl. The flooring of the shed was dirt, too, and it hadn't been baked, not like that on the outside. So, once under the wall, the rest was a bit easier.

I dug and pushed and pushed and dug and finally, my hand pushed into the open space inside the shed. "You through?" Grady asked.

I said I was.

He grabbed my ankle and pulled me out of the hole and in he went. Grady was always bigger, so I let him push me around more than I should have.

After a final bit of digging, I heard Grady's exclamation of "Wow!" coming from inside the shed. Then in a second, his head appeared in the hole. "You coming or not?"

"Your daddy's gonna shoot us," I said.

"You got that right," Grady said. "Cause that's what he's got stored in here--guns!"

"Really?"

"Come on, pokey." And he disappeared inside the shed.

I followed. I knew this was going to get me my obligatory whipping. I was doing two bad things. First, breaking into Uncle Beau's shed. And second, I was getting my clothes dirtier than I thought possible. By the time I crawled into the interior of the shed, I was coated with red dirt, top to toe. But once inside, I forgot all about that.

Grady stood in the middle of the small room with a huge rifle in his hands. I heard him slip the bolt and saw the boxes of shells. Had he put a cartridge into place? "Look it this," he said.

I looked. There was some sort of strange looking writing on the wood stock of the ugly gun. "Can you read that?" I asked.

"Hell, no." I was in the worst trouble of my life. Grady was using cuss words. And he was fiddling with a gun that Uncle Beau didn't want fiddled with. It was clear why he had that lock in place. It was to keep kids away from these dangerous things.

"You know what I think this is?" Grady said.

"What."

"I betcha this is Japanese."

"You think?"

"Yeah. My Daddy was stationed in Japan for a long time after the war," he said.

"So was mine."

"But my daddy was in the Army." He pointed the gun at the door and blew air out his mouth in a kind of childish explosion.

"My daddy was in the Navy."

"Yeah. Too bad," he said. "Wanna play war?"

"I think you better put that thing down. Could be loaded."

"You're such a scaredy cat." He put it down anyway and rummaged among the boxes and crates that were stacked in the room. Then he let out another huge "Wow!!" and pulled a large knife from among the boxes.

"You know what this is, don't you?" he said.

"A butcher knife."

"You're so stupid. It's a bayonet."

The size of the word was impressive. Bay-yo-net. "What's it for?"

"My daddy's told me all about bayonets and things. You hook it on the end of your rifle so when you run out of bullets you can fight off the Japs with the blade."

"Wow," I said, awed.

"Turns your gun into a spear."

"Wooooow."

There was more to be found. Our "Wows" became bigger and bigger. There was a stack of Japanese paper money, a box of strange coins some with holes in the middle, so many boxes of bullets for the five guns we found that we figured Uncle Beau was ready to start fighting the Japs all over again. And then we found the real treasure, something that even Grady knew was bad and wrong to have anything to do with: a carton of brown and ugly Japanese cigarettes. As Grady pulled the carton from a large crate, the cardboard gave way, scattering the cigarettes all over the floor. "Your daddy's gonna kill us," I said, edging toward the hole.

"You ever smoked a cigarette?" he asked.

"Sure," I lied.

"When?"

"Last year."

"Where?"

"Behind my Granny Bea's house."

"Who with?"

"I don't know." I couldn't think fast enough.

"You're lying."

"Am not."

"Liar liar pants on fire."

"I'll go tell your daddy that you're in here messing with his stuff."

"You wanna try one?"

". . . No. . ."

"You a sissy."

"Am not."

"Sissy sissy fraid of whisky."

"Am not."

"Then smoke one with me."

He lit a cigarette using a Japanese lighter he found among the memorabilia. At least, he tried to light a cigarette. The thing wouldn't take the flame.

I'd watched Howie smoke lots of times. So I said, "You got to suck in."

"I know that." So Grady sucked in and the ugly cigarette flared like a torch. He coughed. And the cigarette was lit. He took a pull and coughed again. "Great," he said, turning all kinds of red in the face. "You try."

Both my parents smoked all the time, so it couldn't be all that bad. It didn't seem to bother them any. So I took the lit cigarette and pulled smoke into my mouth the way Howie did. Oh Lord, did that thing burn. It felt as if my whole head had caught on fire, and I spat it out, needing water to remove the rancid taste from my mouth.

"Sissy," Grady said as he lit a second cigarette, and pulled the smoke into his mouth with greater care. "You have to inhale it," he said, and nearly choked.

I tried again. Not so bad the second time. But it was putrid stuff. I couldn't imagine my parents getting any pleasure out of such things. But then, maybe American cigarettes have a better taste. Maybe that's why these Japanese things were stored away. Just not any good. I tried inhaling the smoke like Grady said and felt my head spin around like a top. The room wouldn't stand still. I coughed and sat down in the middle of the shed, hoping sitting still would stop the room's whirling. But it got worse. And I finally had to admit, "I feel sick!"

And Grady said, "Me too. . ."

"You gonna throw up?"

"Maybe."

We heard the key enter the lock outside the door. We were too sick to stand, too sick to squirm back down the hole. We sat there, smoke ringing our heads, as Uncle Beau yanked open the door to the shed.

"What in God's name--" That was all Uncle Beau said. He reached in, pulled Grady off the ground, and landed a swat on his behind that sent a shower of red dirt swirling in the air. He literally threw Grady through the door. He landed on his rump and rolled in the dirt. "Get in the house, you hear me!" Uncle Beau ordered.

I was too sick to know how scared I was. I felt my whole body come off the ground. I felt a swat on my behind equal to what Grady had received. Only, I felt no pain. I could hear Uncle Beau's voice, bouncing around inside my head, but I couldn't understand anything he was saying.

So Grady and I spent the rest of that afternoon confined to his room. We bathed. Aunt Martha gave me some clean clothes to wear, some of Grady's old things he'd outgrown, as she whispered, "You're such a naughty little boy." And they promised that when my folks came back, I'd surely catch all living hell.

My sick feelings went away quick enough without my actually throwing up. Grady wasn't so lucky. The retching he did was awful to hear.

I sat beside Grady on his bed, listening to the row coming from the kitchen. Martha and Beau were fussing about the shed and its contents. Aunt Martha was saying things like "They could have burned the whole place down," and "They could have shot one another with those guns," and "I told you to get rid of those things, Charlie, and I mean it!" Uncle Beau defended himself by saying such things as "I'll get a bigger lock," and "Those things are valuable, Martha," and so on and so forth. Even though I was only six, I knew Uncle Beau was losing the argument. I also knew without having to be told that Grady and I were in the biggest trouble either of us had ever seen. Anytime you can get adults arguing over what you've done, you know: this thing you did was bad.

When Indella and Howie came to pick me up, there was a lot of whispering coming from the kitchen.

"What you think they're saying?" I asked Grady.

He smirked. "I'll give you three guesses and the first two don't count."

Howie didn't say a thing to me on the way home. That worried me. It wasn't like him to go quiet like that. I was used to him hollering and sending me out for a switch. When we got home, the two adults sat in the front of the Pontiac staring at the road ahead. Strange, too. Neither of them lit up a cigarette. That was weird.

"Go get yourself a hickory stick," he told me.

I got the thickest stick I could find. Howie gave me the switching of my life, not because I had gotten my good clothes filthy or because I had broken into Uncle Beau's shed without permission. He whipped me for having anything to do with a loaded rifle. And then he let me have it for smoking. That confused me. I mean, after all, he smoked, didn't he?

After the whipping, he lit a cigarette and lectured for over thirty minutes on the evils of smoking.

When Howbo, who had spent the day at Granny Bea's helping her get some tomatoes ready for canning, asked me what I had done that had stirred up so much trouble, I answered: "Nothing."

3

So, here you are, Howell Madison Cobb, hating the life you lead outside your home. You're already past thirty, well past your prime, and everything around you is hateful and you are afraid that what you have dreamed for yourself and your family is unattainable and you are filled with longing.

This thing: your family. Indella and Howbo and the little sissy Winston and the sickly Trudy. You hadn't counted on a wife and three kids. But thank God for them. They are what give meaning to everything you do. They cause you to consider things in their proper relationship. And you know: how you treat your wife and kids at home is directly related to how you are treated at work. And you hate every bit of it. Must change. Eight years is long enough. Too long. Omiya has slipped into that category occupied by name only: her face has left you. You can't recall the touch of her hand or the tone of her words, words you couldn't understand, the solace you felt in her presence. All has left you with an emptiness. Add that to the failure of your ability to provide adequately for your family and you have cause for change.

It isn't easy talking to your wife. She is too much in admiration of you to listen appropriately. You wish she would grow up. Or at least, act like an adult when you are around. Her sweetness is beautiful, but it is a barrier, too. You want to discuss some difficult things with her, but she refuses. Instead, she says: Whatever you want, sweetheart.

Like the time you brought home the new Pontiac. Instead of lambasting you with harangues about how dare you spend money we don't have, she praises you for your good taste in colors. You hate green. The reason you bought a green car was because it was the only one on the lot that you felt you could afford. And she's praising you!

Like the time you announce that you have to go to Atlanta for a weekend, something to do with a conference of grocers. There wasn't a conference. There weren't any grocers. But she didn't ask. All she said was have fun, hon. And of course you didn't. You sat in a cheap hotel on the edge of Buttermilk Bottoms drinking sour mash from a Mason jar and smoking rancid cigarettes. You didn't even leave your room.

So now. Crisis time in your life and you have to confront your wife and tell her the God awful truth: your sanity is in the balance. How you wish you could chuck it all, say the hell with it and simply disappear. It's been known to happen. Isn't that what Rudy did? Walked out of the Veteran's Hospital and disappeared. Not heard from since except that once, the postcard from a place called Lima. You could do that. Just disappear. If you only knew where Lima was.

But your Momma sits in your head. She's been there all your life, telling you what was proper and what was not. And to desert your wife and kids wasn't in the books, not for you, not for a Cobb. Stay the course, something you've always done, no matter what the cost. Except that once when you left the C's. That was different. That was family.

Well, so is this. Don't go crazy, you've got a family. So there's only one way out: sell the damn grocery store. Get the hell out of hell. Maybe that will help.

You put it off until putting it off any longer would be a disaster. You wait until you and your wife are lying in bed and you've had your way with her. As always, she had lain there like a concubine, her presence, her physical act of breathing her only contribution. She made no sounds, she gave no indications if what you were doing was what she liked or disliked. She was simply there and when it was over, she as usual asked, "Can I get you anything?"

"Got something to tell you," you say.

"Okay."

"Something serious."

"Okay."

You tell Indella that if you stay in the grocery business one more week you're going crazy, that she'll have to have you committed to Milledgeville and will have to visit you on weekends and you'll be there until you turn sixty if you don't put a bullet through your head before then.

"You wouldn't do that," she says.

"What? Do what?"

"Put a bullet-- we don't have a gun."

You determine that tomorrow you're buying that single-shot twenty-two that Pierson's been trying to pawn off on you for the past month. You can say you want to take up hunting. But you'll know why it'll be in the house. And so will she.

"I hate the store," you say.

"So what's wrong with the grocery store?" she wants to know. It's given her and the kids a decent life, not everything she wants but certainly everything she needs. She is proud, she says, to be married to a prosperous grocery store owner and isn't there anything she can do to help you?

You tell her the truth: You can't stand a business where credit is not only expected but assured. You can't say no to folks you grew up with when they come to you with sob stories wanting credit. You show her: the ledger is filled with IOUs from closest friends to relatives to total strangers. You're owed more than two months groceries not by a few but by a bunch, by just about everybody you know. There's even an outstanding bill from your older brother, Hev that's seven months past due. And you don't know what to do about it. And on top of that, you can't keep good help. You keep missing money from the till and you're sure it's winding up in your cashier's pocketbook. And the stock boys are worthless, putting the soda crackers in with the string beans and the canned tuna in with the ice cream. It wouldn't be so bad, but it's been this way since the beginning, and you need a change.

"The boys'll be big enough to help out soon."

"Can't wait that long," you say.

"What do you want to do about it?" Indella asks.

"Sell," you say. It's the first time you've actually put the word out there for someone to hear and it feels right. The right thing to do. "Sell, the sooner the better."

"Who to?" she asks.

You grin. You'd hoped she'd ask. "Hev wants the place," you tell her. "Willing to take it off my hands, set me free."

"To do what?"

You want to say ,Move to Japan, find Omiya, regain your life. But you know better. Your whole family's here in Douglasville and the Village. Every last one of them's moved no more than a few miles away. Even Pierson, home from the war with a silver plate in his head from Pearl Harbor and a noticeable limp in his left leg from Normandy and a severe drinking problem from trying to make his body feel better, lives in his old room in May Lou

and *Alexander Stevens Cobb's house. He's the one with Happy Feet and he's home to stay. So, the question: "And Do What?" Has no answer.*
Except:
   "Move. For now."
   "To where?" she asks.
   You take in a deep breath and let it out slow. "Found us a place in the country," you tell her, "out in Bill Arp Community. A farm."
   The look of disappointment in Indella's eyes is exactly what you'd expect. She's a city girl, lived inside the city limits of Douglasville all her life. She doesn't know anything at all about country living except the biases she carries based on what she has come to associate with country hicks. She is shaking her head no as she whispers, "A farm?"
   "Eighty three acres. A creek. Pasture land for cows and timber for the kids to explore. And a house and a barn--"
   "A house?"
   "Big old rambling house built before the War," you say.
   "Which War? The one with Japan?"
   "No," you say, hesitant because you have no idea how she's going to deal with the next information. "The Civil War."
   "Oh," she says. "Whatever you want." And that's that.
   "You want to know where it is?"
   "Not really," she says.
   "Out Highway 5 and down Harper's Mill Road two and a half miles and turn on Mason Creek Road about half a mile."
   "Sounds like it's the other side of the moon."
   "Just seven miles is all. Can I take you to see it?"

"Guess so," she says. But there's no enthusiasm behind her words.

Can you do this? You bought the grocery store and tried to make a go of it that way. If you can buy a grocery store, Howie Cobb, you can do just about anything you want. Like be a farmer. A damn good farmer, too, one who is in love with his land. You can do it. You will do it. The sooner the better.

CHAPTER SEVEN
Looking For Change

1

So it came to pass that the Howell Madison Cobb family moved to the country when I was nine and all of us lived Howie's escape. Indella hated the place. It was cold and drafty, ugly and lonesome. I try to remember a time when she was happy in that place far outside the comforts of town, but that memory won't come since it doesn't exist. The main thing I remember about living in the country is of her, crying. Nearly every day I'd see Indella CoraMae Shealy Cobb, washing dishes or fixing dinner or hanging up wet wash, crying, tears running down her face and falling off the tip of her chin. Maybe it was just her hurt eye, watering. Regardless, she didn't wipe the water away. She wanted her tears seen.

There wasn't much about the farm Howie bought that was worth much praise. The house sat on top of a hill and faced a dirt road that ran past the place toward Villa Rica one direction and Bill Arp the other. It had been built right after the Civil War and had withstood nearly a hundred years of tenancy by the time the Howie Cobbs moved in. The front yard was rimmed beside the road by boxwoods, several scrub oak trees, and a prolific pear tree that produced pears so hard you could use them as baseballs. A spacious porch ran along the front of the house, shielded from the road by huge boxwoods. I loved those boxwoods. They made perfect hiding places for "ready or not."

The back yard ran to the pasture fence and encompassed a copse of fruit trees that rarely bore fruit and several huge fig trees. I liked the fig trees most because they made me think the back yard was special, a place where Adam and Eve might have found a comfortable place to live. To one side of the yard was a huge oak tree that gave much needed shade in the summer and a place for the guineas to perch and make their non-stop racket every night of the year. Along the back of the house was another rambling porch, similar to the one in front. Before we moved from the place, over half of the back porch had been walled in with a room for Trudy, a new indoor bath, and a utility room where the freezer stayed. The rest of the porch remained as a place for sitting on cool afternoons, a perfect spot to admire the many beautiful sunsets that came our way.

Inside were two bedrooms to begin with. The three kids occupied one, the other belonging to Howie and Indella. There were fireplaces in all rooms, the only source of heat in the winter. A hallway opened from the front door into the two bedrooms and a sitting room, which served for quite some time as a third bedroom. Then there was the kitchen, center of life on the farm. I remember the linoleum that covered the floor: since there was no underpinning to the house, the wind, when it blew, would lift the linoleum free of the floor so that when you walked on it, you could feel the breeze from outside rushing up your legs. One of the first things Howie did to improve the place was fix that underpinning.

When we first moved in, there were two single-seat outhouses in back. It took a while to get used to squatting in an outhouse. There was no running water inside the house. That was the second thing Howie took care of.

Across the dirt road was the barn, a small but sturdy structure made of unhewed logs stacked on top of one another. That barn was my favorite place on the farm: the loft was a treasure of smells and places to hide and find solitude. Several animals came with the farm: a milk cow, a plow horse and mule, a turkey gobbler with several hens, a number of game chickens, a flock of guineas, and a hound or two.

And I loved it. At the same time, Indella hated it. She let her husband know in no uncertain terms just how much she despised living so far from Glory Bea. Too far to walk, too far to visit. Too far, that was all there was to it.

"But we're here," Howie reasoned. "We're settled."

"You may be settled. I ain't." And she'd go away to cry some more.

The money Howie Cobb made when he sold the grocery store didn't last long. But that didn't matter to him since the purpose for buying land in the country was to make a living off it. With the house and the barn and handful of farm animals came a bit more than eighty acres of red colored earth. Over half the acreage was in woods, the other half in pasture land. We could stand on our back porch and see the stretch of our land: from here to that row of trees beyond the field. To Howie Cobb, it must have felt good, seeing how much he now owned.

The problem was he didn't know how to go about making a living off the land. He came from a long line of mill workers for whom mill working was all they knew. Being a grocer as he had been was an easy shift; everybody needed groceries, simple enough. But farming. Now that was something Howie Cobb had to learn from scratch. And we learned it right along side of him.

First thing: fence in the pastures, both sides of the road. Howbo and I were the only help Howie had until Donkey Shedd showed up and he proved to be virtually worthless. And the work was hard, so much so that Howbo proclaimed most every night: "Never gonna be a farmer, not in this lifetime or the next." Digging holes for fence posts was the thing that just about did both of us in. The red clay that some folks called soil was baked hard as brick by the unrelenting Georgia sun. Howbo would get the posthole started with the post hole diggers and then I'd come along with the water bucket and empty the liquid into the hole. The dirt was mostly rocks so the going was tortuous. Howbo and I wanted to quit more times than we could count, but Howie Cobb would hear nothing of it. Got to get the fence posts in and the hog wire strung cause Mr. Daniels, neighbor to the west, was gonna rent our pasture land for his herd of Jersey heifers. If that wasn't enough, my chore every morning and evening was milking Melba, the cow that had come with the farm. Howbo had to take care of the rest of the animals, but he didn't complain about that. Milking had to be done before seven every morning and after six in the early evening. I learned the meaning of hard work by the time I was ten.

Indella became sadder than a widow deserted by her friends. The farm was a bit more than seven miles from the Douglasville she had grown up in, but those seven miles were as good as a hundred when it came to getting into town or having relatives come visit. I remember the time that Aunt Martha and Grady came calling. It was quite the thing, having visitors. I got to show Grady all the special places of the farm, and he loved it!

"You're so damn lucky Pooh," he said, and meant it. "Look at all you got to do out here!"

I wanted to say, 'you can have it all, buddy, and every fence post on the place'. I let him "Ooh" and "Ahh" all he wanted.

That was the only visit I remember. It wasn't enough, not for Indella Cobb. But more than enough for Howie who made a point of noting how few of the Douglasville folk ever came to call.

2

Saturday afternoons during summer vacation after Little League baseball practice, I sat on the red banks of the Bill Arp Elementary School playing field and scanned the skies with binoculars and listened for the steady drone of airplanes. It was a vigil that was a community engagement.

It was 1954.

Somehow or other we got involved in the Civil Defense for Bill Arp Community, which meant we hung around the school house long after baseball practice and passed binoculars back and forth. That's not quite accurate. I was too young to be involved with binoculars. My role was that of begging just for a brief peek through the special instruments.

It was the summer that I sat around scanning the skies for planes and Howie made fun of Hoyt Statum for spending thousands of dollars building a fallout shelter in the middle of his back yard.

Hoyt, a food supplier whom Howie had met during his days in the grocery store, lived in Cedartown. When the family visited Hoyt and his wife Mary one Sunday afternoon, the proud owner of the new concept for surviving a nuclear war gave all of us a tour of what he had built himself. "With the sweat of my brow," he was fond of saying. The hole in the ground a hundred or so feet from his back door had a mud floor, walls reinforced with two by four studs, and a tin ceiling. You entered the shelter through a hinged trap cut in the tin and inched down a rickety homemade ladder. Once inside, you found exactly what Hoyt had intended: a hole in the ground, nothing more. It was large enough to accommodate three people as long as the three didn't care about moving around very much and standing was the preferred posture. With Hoyt,

Mary, and their two daughters, I wondered who would be left outside when the bombs started falling.

"Not got it stocked yet," Hoyt said and pointed to places where he anticipated adding shelving and indicated the beginnings of another hole-like cave where he planned to store perishables. There was no drainage system in case it rained. I was curious: what if somebody had to go to the bathroom? I wanted to ask, but I knew from Howie's lack of questions that some things were not really welcome. When the three of us had squeezed inside leaving a skeptical Howbo outside and Hoyt had closed the trap door, the hole was thrown into darkness. Howie struck a match to light a cigarette and Hoyt borrowed it long enough to ignite a kerosene hurricane lamp that hung from one of the three rafters supporting the tin ceiling. The lamp threw strange shadows on the red clay walls.

I faintly recall Hoyt being unusually proud of his fallout shelter, patterned, he said, after the specs he found for such constructions in a Civil Defense pamphlet. I also remember feeling claustrophobic in the tiny hole, like I had entered a grave without the comfort of death or a casket. Fallout shelters and being buried alive have much in common.

"What use is a fallout shelter?" Howie asked Hoyt when we crawled back up the ladder.

Hoyt's reply was snippy. "It's my money, I'll spend it how the hell I please."

Howie got the message: say anything more about Hoyt's fallout shelter and he would risk destroying a treasured friendship.

Howie and Indella held a family discussion after that visit to Cedartown. Howie told us how much a shelter on your farm would cost and Indella said, "Is there a price on the health and safety of your children?"

"You have no idea of what an atomic bomb can do to a place," Howie said.

"And you do I suppose?"

The words were ready to flow out of him. Instead, he said, "Let's discuss this later."

"Now seems like a good time to me," Indella said. "For instance, should you stock up on store-bought canned vegetables and boxes of soda crackers? Or would the mason jars of beets, apple sauce, and stewed tomatoes be enough?"

"What about fresh air--how do you get the stench of wet earth out of the hole?" I asked. I had been down there. I knew how musty the place smelled.

"And where would you go to the bathroom?" Howbo asked. "Should you take toilet paper with you or leave it outside?"

"Sorry, folks," Howie said. "No fallout shelter's being built on this farm."

"I'd like to know why not," Indella said.

"What would you do," Howie asked her, "if we were the only people in the whole of Bill Arp to own a fallout shelter--and we would be if we built one--and a bomb exploded in--say Atlanta--and the family trucked down into that God awful hole-in-the-ground and we were comfortable and all that and then somebody, say Tom and Marveen Duke, who don't have a shelter, came knocking on our door wanting in? What would you say to them, Del?"

She said, "Let them in, of course."

"But we built it just for us! Room enough for the five of us and nobody else. We let in the Duke family and we'd run out of food and air and then every last one of us--you, me, the kids, the Dukes--would die. That's not why you build a fallout shelter, you know--to die. You build it in order to survive. So, what you're telling me is that it would be futile to build us a fallout shelter since we'd die anyway. It doesn't make sense, Del."

Then Indella said, "You just don't love us as much as Hoyt Statum loves his family."

Howie fumed at that remark. He had no retort available when she reduced an argument to its fundamental human form. So he tried another approach. He said, "Think about it this way. Let's say we build us a fallout shelter and Atlanta is hit and we lock ourselves away for as long as it takes, say a year or so. They say, fallout can take even longer than that before it's at a safe level. Anyway, we're the only people in Bill Arp to own such a shelter and after a year we come out, assuming we can survive that long. Have you ever thought what the world would be like? If a bomb hit Atlanta, there won't be much left. We'd come out and everywhere we'd look would be empty, a nuclear desert. All our neighbors'd be dead. All the livestock would be dead. Trees, grass, everything gone. We'd have nothing to eat, and we'd be miserable until we, too, were dead. Is that the kind of life you'd wish on yourself and your children?"

"Sounds okay to me," Howbo said with a grin.

"I promise you, it's not. People dying all around you from radiation sickness. It's a horrible way to die. Your hair falls out. Then your skin turns yellow, then purple. You puke up blood--"

"All right, Howie, we understand!" Indella said. "Nobody in their right mind would make a bomb that would do such a thing to the world as that."

Howie put an end to the discussion when he said, "Who says the people building bombs here and in Russia are in their right minds?"

There were maps published in newspapers showing possible enemy nuclear targets, giving the prioritization for such targeting, and possible fallout patterns with high, medium, and low intensity areas distinguished by coded shading. Atlanta was listed as a second to third priority target, meaning, I suppose, that Denver, Colorado, Washington D.C. and Rapid City, South Dakota would be blown up before anybody got hit in Georgia. According to the map, Douglas County was a high-risk area for fallout, due to receive the most severe dosage of any Atlanta suburb, if the city were hit. That meant that everybody living in Bill Arp Community would be killed either instantly by the blast or within a few months from radiation sickness. Such predictions made me want to agree with Indella: Who in their right minds . . .

3

They're beautiful birds on the fly. They gather the wind on a kind of mattress and float way up there, sometimes nothing more than dots of charcoal against white clouds. You'd never know they were anywhere around but for their high, piercing hawk-sound, something like a child's tin whistle. Today such a sound creates nostalgia. Back then, it caused concern: the damn chicken hawks are out again.

I was the chicken farmer in the family. At nine, I had my first 4-H project: a "brace" of Japanese chickens. At nine and a half, I progressed to a flock of Rhode Island Reds (a hundred chicks, meant to be egg-machines). I learned to be wary of the chicken hawk at a very early age.

I remember standing in our backyard, scanning the skies, looking for the bird that made that eerie sound. The whistle came from where the hawk had been, not where it was. There it would be, a tiny speck circling like a kite, moving without effort, its wide wings cupping the air, floating with an ease that invited envy.

Howie stood beside me. I'd never seen the hawk actually take any chickens, but I had noticed one or more of my 4-H flock missing. "I remember once," Howie said, "my Uncle Sol took care of a chicken hawk. I was about your age, Winston."

"How?"

"Shot it right out of the sky with a twenty two."

"He must have been quite a shot."

"My Uncle Sol could do just about anything, son. Shoot a gun better than most, play poker better than most, get drunker and meaner than most. What do you think," he said, both of us staring at the speck of a bird high above the farm. "Think we can get him?"

"I bet you can," I said.

"Be right back," he said and entered the house.

I continued to follow the bird's circular pattern. Though a predator of my 4-H brood and the domestic stock of game hens and roosters as well an occasional guinea hen, those loud speckled-gray things that roosted nightly outside our bedroom windows and kept all awake until well past ten, I couldn't help admiring the hawk. It soared so far above my head I had difficulty keeping it in focus. Yet from its lofty vista, it could spot a field mouse as it breathed.

Howie returned with his rifle, an implement I wasn't allowed to touch. Howbo came with him. It wasn't often that Howie took his rifle off the rack. It was something of a treat.

"Okay," he said, "where's the pigeon?" Howbo and I both pointed. The hawk continued its lazy circle, still a mere flyspeck on the sky's ceiling.

"Let me try," Howbo said. And he did. Boom. The hawk was unconcerned, it's whistle sounding slightly like a taunt.

"What you've got to do," Howie said, "is lead it. Aim where you expect the bird to be when the bullet gets there."

"How much of a lead?"

"Let me show you." Howie took aim. Boom. Everybody watched. The hawk was taunting still for a second, then. . . it's circling developed a hitch, like a blip on a heart monitor or something. It dipped, not a great deal, but some, before it began its descent.

"Hey!" Howbo said, filled with pride for his father's marksmanship. "I think you got him!"

All of us watched in awe as the chicken hawk's grand flight pattern became that of a crippled plane like those in World War Two movies. It started down in a spiral, dipping, sometimes re-establishing a soar, then down, down, down. . .

We watched it into the woods on the other side of the pasture. "Damn," Howie said, "I didn't know I could do that." There was a strange look on his face, one I'd not seen before. But I was too excited to pay any attention to such things then.

"I want to go find him," Howbo said. So, off we went, on what both of us considered a dangerous mission. It was like looking for a downed Russian pilot hiding somewhere in our back forty.

By the time we returned from the woods with the bird in hand, Howie Cobb had gone. Nobody knew where. Not even Indella. According to her, he had put the rifle in the back of the pick-up, cranked it and without saying good-bye, backed out of the driveway, and drove down Mason Creek Road toward Villa Rica, raising a cloud of dust.

He'll be back for supper, she said.

Little did she know.

CHAPTER EIGHT
Free At Last, Never Free, Free At Last

1

You didn't anticipate this. Your first impulse was to take a drive, you didn't care where to or for how long. Just take a drive. The old pick-up was there and you got in it and before you knew it, you were in Bremen, heading west.

In your head, you're on board that damn ship again, in the middle of the Pacific, in the middle of a war, squatting beside that little Japanese fellow, offering him a piece of Spearmint gum and telling him about the chicken hawk your Uncle Sol had shot and that you had let starve to death. Too much. Go for broke, as they used to say, only that was about the Marines, wasn't it? You don't know. You don't care.

Birmingham is an ugly place.

Hate the damn city. Too many people in too small a place. So you don't stay.

Meridian. Too damn hot. Where's home? Are the kids okay?

You hate the idea of killing things, even a chicken hawk that's not out to hurt anyone. Simply doing its thing, soaring a mile or more above the ground, looking for anything that moves. You had no right to do that. None.

It's morning when you reach Monroe. How did you get here? Does it matter? Which way do you go to get home?

Home.

Do you really know?

What's home when you have no earthly idea where the hell you are. . .

2

The hawk was in the chicken coop Howie had built the summer before as a place to hold day-old chicks while the shed was being readied. It was surprising how small a hawk can be when it's up close and you can stare into its eyes. Are we as small as it, really? Just as small if not smaller?

"Where's your father?" Indella asked.

"I bet he needed more cartridges for his gun," Howbo said. He's always going into town for one thing or another. It's his way of relaxing. I've known that about him for almost a year now. Sometimes I'd hop into the cab of the pickup to ride along, a good way to spend time with him when usually he doesn't want anybody around. Once he'd let me behind the wheel and I'd promptly run the pickup into the ditch. He'd cursed at me about that, and I didn't like it, being cursed at. I didn't ask to drive the pickup again, not after that.

"Well, if you see him, tell him. . ." It was obvious she didn't know what it was she wanted us to tell him.

The hawk wouldn't eat. We fed it a head of lettuce from the garden, but everybody knew hawks don't eat vegetables. They eat meat. Live meat.

So without telling Indella, I took the hawk the sick chick I'd been trying to doctor back to health. Actually, the chick wasn't sick at all. It was simply dying. Unable to eat. Stupid chicken. It was only two weeks old, but it had hopped up on the feed sack and started pecking at the string that sealed the sack shut. It had pecked and pecked until it had the string wrapped tightly around and under its tongue. I'd found the sick chick, dangling over the side of the sack, hanging limp by its tongue, still alive if you could call it that. I'd tried untangling the string, trying in every way to get the tongue free of its attachment to the feed sack. I pulled until it looked as if all the chicken's guts were going to come flowing up its gullet. I couldn't stand making the sick chick worse by gutting it while it lived. The string was too tightly wound to come free. So I'd cut the chicken loose and knew it would die, being unable to eat. It was natural, then, to feed this particular chicken to the hawk.

The hawk wasn't interested. It just sat there, eyes deep and penetrating but slowly becoming empty. It ignored the sick chick, almost as if it wasn't even there. Almost as if the hawk itself wasn't there but was still up in the sky, soaring.

I visited the coop after dark with a flashlight, hoping that under cover of darkness the hawk would take the sick chick and make a meal of it. No such luck. The chicken was dead. Untouched by the hawk. It had simply died as I knew it would.

I wanted to reach inside and relieve the hawk of having to share the coop with a dead chicken. But I was too afraid. What if the hawk decided my hand and fingers were the delicacy he really wanted. What if he grabbed hold of me with its long talons. What if the hawk started flopping about like it had when we had found it in the woods, wounded and trying to regain flight. There in the woods, it had been easy enough. I had taken my jacket like Howbo had said and flopped it over the hawk's head, while Howbo grabbed both its feet and yanked it off the ground. Like a turkey hung upside down ready for the swipe of the butcher's knife.

There with just a flashlight and no Howbo to help and the close quarters of the coop I knew it was hopeless. I wouldn't be able to get my jacket over the bird if I'd wanted to.

Indella had crept up behind me. I didn't know she was there until she was there. She had been crying. She'd been crying almost constantly since dinner and Howie hadn't come back from town. Howbo had tried to perk her up by telling her all about the hunt for the hawk but that had made her cry even harder and she'd left the supper table without clearing the food or dishes. And that had made Trudy cry. I don't like it when anybody cries, but when two people do, well I have to cry, too. I had sat at the supper table and bawled, and Howbo had slammed his fork to the table and gone to the barn where he sat with the cows and hogs and more than likely pouted. Nobody seemed to like his story of the chicken hawk hunt.

So Indella stood there, hugging her arms tightly across her chest as if she was cold. "You should let that animal go," she said softly, as if she cared one way or another. "Every creature on God's green earth deserves its freedom," she whispered. I could tell: she wasn't thinking about the hawk.

"At least let me try," I said, not sure I would succeed in keeping the animal alive.

"Let him go, Pooh," she said. "There's some things you simply can't keep locked up." And she turned back to the house where I figured she'd cry herself to sleep, waiting for Howie to come home.

Somehow I knew, even though you shouldn't know such things when you're a kid of just-turned ten. Maybe it's the same as my knowing about the car accident, a premonition. Regardless, I knew: when my Daddy left in the pickup that afternoon, it was because he didn't know where he was going. And now that he was gone, more than likely he didn't know where he was. I also knew he would find his way back to me some day. I didn't know how long it would be, but he'd be back. I had been as sure of that as I had that the chicken hawk wouldn't die.

I left the wire door to the coup standing open hoping the hawk would find itself free.

It didn't. It died instead.

3

My dear wife, Your husband is a fool. He thought he was rushing backward into what he hoped would be answers when in fact he was fleeing awkwardly into more questions. It felt at first as if he was flying with the blessings of God when instead he was charging into a hell, led by the other omniscient being. He is a fool. Always will be.

He had been attracted to something, let's call it "power," or at worse "force." The "force" drained him, leaving him an empty hull. He had hoped the "Power" would fill him with all that he lacked.

Foolish man indeed.

He drove like the devil himself across Alabama, Louisiana, Texas and discovered himself in the bowels of the deserts of New Mexico, devoid of human feelings, "the Valley of Death." It had been here, he discovered, in spite of himself, that the first expression of modern power was made. He had been drawn here as by a magnet or as a moth to an open flame. He didn't understand why. Perhaps it had everything to do with Omiya and Noriko from his days of yore, his days of wandering the atomic field of Hiroshima. Here, he wandered instead the atomic field of the moonscape, hollowed to the core by an overwhelming sense of loss and regret.

Do you, his ever trusting and faithful wife, understand? It was the "power," the expression of "Man as God," the need for fall-out shelters and Civil Defense, that caused him to flee to such a place, to a realm of awesome and idiotic gore. He had seen its finger print at Hiroshima and been appalled. Here, he was awed, as he had somehow expected to be.

How can you, his ever trusting and faithful wife, understand? Understanding is as far from him as believing in a God other than Man. Pray for him, dear wife, for this husband needs much careful and genuine expression of faith.

When there at the site of the first "sun on earth," it was inevitable that this unfaithful husband would find his way north to the brain of cataclysm. This he did with little need for a map of any sort. The pull of power was all he required.

At Los Alamos, he found that they needed test rats, and he volunteered and signed on, only as long as the pay was sufficient and the cause profound. (The checks you receive in the mail are manifestations of my devotion as a laboratory rat.) At last, he had found his station in life: a testee, all white and willing to sacrifice its meager self for the good of all rat-kind. Test rats, you see, have little say in the quality of life they inherit. They live inside glass cages, with test lines run to all parts of their anatomies, nothing they do or think or articulate is too insignificant for the testers to observe and pass on to others inside encrypted notes, safe and secure. This is the life your foolish husband found on the far side of the earth, drawn, he must admit, by the image of Omiya that was slipping inevitably from his test-brain rat's life.

How can such a foolish being explain to you in words that have meaning what it was that extracted him from his life of farmer, of parent, of husband, into a world of such horror and inhumanity? He cannot offer such an explanation. It defies him. It leaves him emptier than before the explanation became necessary. It emptied him of his human and subsequent familial concerns. It left him, instead, endowed with a singular and all defining word: "Vow." Yes, he took an oath stronger than the one pronounced in Ringgold in the presence of Hev and Marlys. He vowed to secrecy, so profound that if he shared even the smallest entity of that which he had accepted, he would be in violation of his devotion to State. Forget God and family and all that other secondary stuff. STATE exceeds all other values and manipulates everything else. It is a matter of "National Security." That is the phrase bandied about and accepted by all who come within its grasp. Your foolish husband was one who took that oath, to his ultimate and most profound chagrin.

Your foolish husband is writing this too foolish letter, one that will more than likely be determined unsendable by powers greater than himself, while under the influence of too many whiskeys at the too undependable bar on this remarkably dependable enclave referred to as "The Place." So if this remarkably unreliable document finds its way to you, please keep this under consideration: your foolish husband is not responsible.

He joined "The Cattle Squad." The fact that the government would accept an ancient swabbie is an indication of the crying need the government has to do the undoable, to test the untestable, to experience the unexperienceable. That is what he, your foolish husband, has sworn to do, and is doing.

It is "D for Detonation Day plus one." Tomorrow will be the final and ultimate examination for rat-brains like your foolish husband's. He will be in touch. He will try to be in touch. Regardless, you are receiving the checks, aren't you?

4

By the end of the first week, Indella was in the church sanctuary every time it was open: Monday night brotherhood, Wednesday evening prayer meeting, Thursday night choir practice, and both Sunday morning and evening services. At each gathering, her prayer was the same: "Dear Lord Jesus, return my husband to me. If it be your will."

will."

Nothing came of her prayers.

After a week of no word of any sort, Indella called Marlys and invited her to the farm for a visit. It was a distance for Marlys to travel, but she recognized the agony in Indella's voice and knew it was important for her to attend to her sister-in-law's plea for help. The actual words, "I need help," weren't there, but she heard the tone of voice that spoke louder than any words possible.

"Howie's gone," Indella told her one and only friend.

"To the store?" Marlys offered.

"I mean, for good."

Marlys sensed the depth of emotion her dear friend and fellow "war widow" was feeling. "Tell me," she said, simply and without reserve.

"Last week," Indella said, "Howie and the kids shot a chicken hawk. And within just a couple of minutes, Howie was in the pick up truck and gone. We ain't heard from him since."

"What did he take with him?" Marlys asked.

"Just his rifle."

"No clothing, nothing to eat?"

"Just what clothes he had on his back."

Marlys was hesitant to ask such sensitive things, but it seemed important to know all one could. "What about money?"

"Oh, I'm fine, sweetheart. You don't need to worry about that."

"No," Marlys said, "I mean on him? Did he take a lot of money with him?"

"Just what he had in his pocket. I don't know."

"You ain't heard from him for over a week?"

"No," was the only word available to Indella under such scrutiny. She wanted to say that Howie was just down the road apiece, looking for some way to get in touch. But she knew this wasn't the case. She knew Howie was gone to a far and distant world. It was the same world that had dragged him away from the grocery business a few months back, and it was the same urge that was luring him into worlds unknown.

Marlys remained calm, in spite of the feelings she had inside her. Feelings of revolt, of 'I'll be damned in hell before I'll forgive this.' "You want me to call Hev?" she asked.

"Lord, no!" Indella exclaimed. She was protecting her good husband's name, assuming he still had one.

"What then?"

"Marlys, I'm at a total loss, I swear I am," Indella said. The child inside her was slowly slipping away and in its place, a precise and rather commanding adult was taking shape. She wasn't sure of herself yet, but it was slowly beginning to manifest itself, that self that emerges under dire straits.

"Maybe he's been in an accident," Marlys suggested.

"I would have heard. Don't you think I would have heard?"

"One would think." She leaned forward, placing a comforting hand on Indella's knee. "Maybe he's been in touch with somebody in the family."

"Oh, I hope not," Indella said, her back straightening in defiance. The idea of Howie deserting her and then bragging about it to his brothers and sisters, or worse, to Momma Cobb, was the height of degradation. That would be something beyond forgiveness, assuming that at some point in the future Howie returned to her, hat in hand.

"So," Marlys said a word that expressed itself as she let the air out of her lungs. "What do you propose that we do, Indella?"

"We?" she asked.

"You don't think you're in this thing alone, do you?"

"I wasn't sure," she said, feeling somehow relieved, somehow ready to face the next step, whatever that might be.

"Family is one," Marlys said.

And that was all it took for Indella to recognize who she was and what her rights as a human being really were. She took Marlys by the hand and held her tight. "Thank you," she whispered, her soul finding its first moments of freedom. "Thank you, my dear friend," she said.

5

Howbo and I were needed, whether we knew it or not. We were suddenly thrust into positions of having to do, no questions asked. The cows were milked, the stock fed, the eggs collected, the fields fertilized, the fences mended, everything it fell to us to do.

Howie had prepared us well. I knew the beginning and ending of my chores; Howbo knew his. And we did them.

Indella took care of the rest: the kitchen stuff, the cleaning, and the laundry, the urging us to get down the hill in order to catch the bus to school.

School wasn't much those days. My mind was occupied with Howie's disappearance. Where might he have gone? And why?

It was our secret. As far as I knew, Indella told no one. Neither did I. Howbo and I talked about it and decided between us that the less that other folks knew the better for us all.

Indella was suffering. That much was plain. She didn't know what to do next in terms of making the farm work for us. It was Howbo who stepped up. He may not have understood everything that needed doing, but he convinced her that he did. I was in awe of my older brother and hoped that someday I'd get to be as smart as he. Howbo stepped up and became for us all the new "Howie." That comes, I guess, with being the first born.

"Howie," I wanted to say, as loud and as clear as I possibly could, "Where ever you are, stay there. We don't need you!" But deep inside, I knew this wasn't the truth. I was only ten and Howbo was only twelve. We needed our Daddy. Desperately.

There was one truth that all of us had to accept: He wasn't there. End of that debate.

Then on the first day of summer vacation from school, something came in the mail, addressed to us all. It was in a brown government envelope, metered, not stamped. Howbo and I were thrilled to finally have the year's schooling behind us and we came into the kitchen filled with plans for the coming months. It was at the kitchen table that we found Indella, the government letter sitting in front of her, unopened.

"What's this?" Howbo said, taking the letter and shaking it near his ear.

"It's to us all," Indella said.

"So open it," Howbo said. Being "man of the house" meant he could treat our mother as his equal. He had no hesitation in ordering her about.

"I don't have the energy," she said, her voice barely above a whisper. I could tell: she believed the envelope contained the direst of news regarding Howie. She, like me, wasn't sure she wanted to know what was inside it.

In The Shelter of The Fold

Silence for the two of us was better than absolutes. I wanted to take the mail from Howbo and drop it in the garbage can, but he already had it open.

"It's a check, Mom," he said, "made out to you. Wow. That's a lot of money! Look it that, Winnie. Holy Toledo."

"Who's it from?" Indella asked.

"The United States of America."

"What's it for?"

"Heck if I know," Howbo said, giving the check to her. "It's made out to you. 'For Deposit Only'."

"There's no letter then?"

"No, ma'am."

"It's from Daddy," I said for no reason whatsoever. It just felt like it was from Howie. It was the sort of thing he had done in the past. It was what I would have done if it had been me.

Obviously my credibility as a seer was unquestioned. Indella said, "I think you're right, Pooh." She seemed saddened by the check. It was as if now we could forget about the possibility of Howie's return. That wasn't going to happen. The check was proof that he had no intention of returning home. He was buying us, securing his freedom through cash. All his responsibility to us, his family, was being compensated for. His guilt was no longer something we could count on bringing him back to us.

"Set down, boys," Indella said. "We've got a decision to make."

"Want me to get Trudy?" I asked. She was on the back porch, playing with Spot, one of the beagle's new puppies.

"No," she said. "This is business. She's too young to be of much help when it comes to business."

I was beaming at that moment. I had just gotten promoted to the fourth grade and there I was, being invited by the grown ups to join in a discussion of family matters. I sat at the table straight and tall, wanting to be absolutely certain that my contributions were manly.

Indella began. "Your daddy's not coming home, not any time soon."

"You've heard from him?" Howbo asked.

"Just this check, son, nothing else." She folded the check and put it in her purse. "I'm going into town and deposit this in the morning. I'd like the two of you, and Trudy, too, to come along."

"Sure," Howbo said. "I'll drive."

"No you won't. All right now. By putting this check in the bank, you know what we're doing, don't you?"

"No, ma'am," I said.

"We're putting Howie Cobb behind us. We're saying that it's just the four of us now, and we've got to start behaving like it."

"You're saying we're to stop hoping he'll come home," Howbo said.

"That's exactly what I'm saying. Are both of you in agreement with that? Now's your chance to have your say."

I spoke first. "I knew the day the chicken hawk died that Daddy wasn't coming back. It felt like he died too."

Then Howbo said, "Even if he does come back, we don't need him. We're just fine the way we are."

"I need him," Indella said, then added, "but I'll get over that eventually." I noticed her hands; they were shaking. And her damaged eye was swimming in liquid. Since the accident, she had difficulties keeping the eye focused. I could see she was struggling with her focus during our conference. "All right, then," she continued. "We are it. It's time that we began acting like we're going somewhere. Now, the first thing is this: I hate this drafty old farmhouse."

"Me, too," Howbo said.

"Me, too," I said.

"I was never a farmer, never had any intention of being one. I'm a city girl, and I swear, boys, I miss living in town."

"Me too," both of us said together.

"What should we do then?" Silence. Howbo fidgeted in his chair. He seemed to know what he wanted to do but was afraid to say it. "Go on, Howbo. What's on your mind?"

"Well, I was thinking that if we lived in town, I could get a job in Uncle Hev's store and earn a little money."

"Me, too," I said.

"You're too young, Pooh. All you'd want to do is work in the candy section."

"Would not."

"Would, too."

"So, Howbo, what about the farm?"

"We could sell it."

There. The words had found time and space. What Howbo had said were the words that none of us thought we had the nerve to say. Sell the farm. Move. Those were two such big words that it took some heavy-duty silence to let them sink in.

It was Indella, her hands no longer shaking, who broke the silence. "You mean that?"

"Yes, ma'am," Howbo said. "I think I do."

"What about the livestock?"

"Sell that, too." Howbo shifted uneasily in his chair. "I never liked living here, Momma. It's creepy."

"You never said anything."

"Why would I? Nobody'd listen."

Indella nodded. It seemed settled. The two huge words, "sell" and "move," didn't seem quite so big any longer. "So, we're selling this place and going home."

"When?" I asked.

"We'll meet with a realtor tomorrow after we go to the bank. We'll sell this place and move in with my Momma until we can get a place of our own. If that's okay with you boys, then we'll do it."

"Okay," said Howbo.

"Okay," I echoed.

And that ended the first family conference to which I had been invited. I felt old all the rest of that day. I had graduated from my childhood ahead of my class.

6

Hank came calling as the family was packing. He parked his car in the front of the house and wandered around back. Nobody saw him come. Nobody saw him go. That was the way he wanted it.

Indella was in the kitchen with stacks of the good china around her. She was wrapping the plates, bowls, cups and saucers, serving platters, and cream dish in newspaper when Hank tapped on the screen door.

"Howdy, sister," he said, that foolish grin on his face, the one that seemed to emerge each time he got around Indella Cobb. "Looks like you're getting ready to move," he said with a sexy laugh.

"Looks like it," she said, not stopping her work.

"Can I come in?"

"What do you want, Hank?" she asked as she slipped the latch to the screen door into place.

"Just being sociable," he said, "come to lend a hand."

"Got all the help I need," she said. "Me and the boys are doing just fine."

He tugged at the door but the latch held. "You're not being very neighborly, Del, keeping your kin standing out in the cold."

"It's eighty-nine degrees, Hank. Nobody's standing in the cold. Go home."

"Wail 'til I tell Howie how his wife treats her in-laws. He ain't gonna like it, no siree Bob."

"You've been in touch with Howie?"

"Sure," he said. "Ain't you?"

"You're lying. You'd do anything to get your way, Hank Cobb. Well, this is one woman who ain't buying." Her hands were quivering and her damaged eye was weeping fluid. She did not need this kind of entertainment, not at this point in her life. It was difficult enough keeping focus on the tasks at hand without Hank coming along to muck things up. "Now if you don't go home, I'll call the sheriff and have him drag you off to the lock up."

"I'm going, I'm going. Howie's gonna be really put out with you, Del. I promise you that."

"Don't care. If you really do know how to get in touch with him, tell him for me I just don't care any more. You tell him that for me, Hank. You tell him."

Indella was shaking all over as Hank stomped down the back porch steps. She realized as she heard the crunch of shattered glass that she had dropped a china plate to the linoleum sometime during her interview with her brother-in-law. She got the broom and dustpan from the closet and swept up the mess. When she rose from the floor, there was Hank Cobb, standing in her way.

"Somebody forgot to lock the front door," he said, that sneering grin on his face. "Let me help you with that." He took the broom and tossed it behind him, and he grabbed her by the neck and pulled her to him. "I like my women to be hard to get," he said.

"I ain't your woman," she said, dropping the dustpan to the floor.

"Not yet, you ain't. But we can remedy that."

He kissed her. He pressed his unshaven mouth over hers and she could taste the whiskey he had used to get up enough nerve to come calling. It was a nasty taste, one she had experienced only once before, that at the hands of her father, Sylvester Shealy. Now, Hank did exactly what Sylvester had done so many years earlier: he thrust his tongue deep inside her mouth. Before, Indella had been too young and naive to know what to do when a man did that to her without her bidding. She was older now. She didn't resist. He held her arms pinned behind her and could feel her ample breasts smashed against his chest. He moaned as his tongue searched for something inside her mouth.

She had read in one of Winston's science books that the muscle inside the jaw is the strongest muscle in the human body. She proved this scientific fact as she brought her teeth together, slicing down and into his meaty tongue and she tasted his hot blood as it filled her mouth. His moan turned to a yelp as he pulled away from her, his hand automatically going to his mouth. "You goddamn bitch," he said. "I ought to break your neck for that."

"I wish you would," she said, her tears of shame flowing freely. The box she had been packing was knocked to the floor, spilling broken and breaking dishes across the linoleum. She intentionally dropped the rest of the dishes to the floor. Screaming incoherently, she fell on top of the mess, beating her open palms into the shards of glass, turning the flooring red with her blood. All she heard were the sounds of her screams, echoing like someone was lost in an empty cave. Hank watched in awe, the pain in his tongue momentarily forgotten. She rose from the floor with pieces of China sticking in her palms, her left little finger all but severed from her hand.

"What in god's name is wrong with you, woman?"

She screamed her answer: "Everything! Everything is wrong! Everything!" She grabbed for a knife from the kitchen sink, but he stopped her, holding her wrists tightly, trying to stop the flow of blood. Her screams became those of a caged animal. They sent shivers of terror up and down Hank's spine. His instinct was to run. Which he did. He tracked blood through the house to his waiting car and drove away, leaving it to Howbo to find his mother, weeping on a pile of broken china, trying to fit the pieces back together.

7

Trudy, Howbo, and I stayed with Granny Bea while Indella was in the hospital. It was too far a drive to go to Milledgeville very often, but we went to visit her every chance we got. It was Hev and Marlys who took us the few times we got to visit. Granny Bea refused to go.

"No member of my family's ever been in an insane asylum," she said as an excuse to stay home.

"Not an insane asylum, Mrs. Shealy," Hev told her. "It's a hospital. It's a place for getting well."

"Got no need for insane asylums," she said.

I spent a lot of time during those days with Junior, Marlys and Hev's second born. Junior and I had fun sharing the adventures of our lives. I told him about the hospital where they kept Indella, and he was eager to hear it all, several times if needed. I told him about how they sewed Indella's little finger back to her hand and about how that finger now just sat there, not moving. It had no feeling left so that Indella chewed on it constantly, causing it to bleed. They dressed her in white during the early part of her stay in the hospital and rolled her around in a wheel chair as if she had lost the use of her legs. They had straps on the chair to keep her from falling out. Once, you told Junior, you had visited your mother and she had done something to her forehead, fallen on it or something because it was wrapped in a bandage that covered most of the top of her head. It made her look a little like Frankenstein. Junior insisted that I show him just how she looked by wrapping his head in a white towel. He was impressed. Later when I saw her head free of the bandage, I saw the circular scar at the edge of her hairline. Her hair had been cut and was as short as mine. That made me think that the doctors were trying to turn her into a man. It made no difference about her hair. She was still a woman, the most beautiful woman I had ever seen.

Usually Indella didn't have much to say during our visits. She asked for Howie, but of course he wasn't around. We kept getting checks from the government, big checks, lots of money, but that was all. When we told her about them, she didn't seem interested. I got the impression that money was the least of her concerns at that time. I told her that the bank was keeping all the money in an account and that it was earning even more money. "We're rich," I tried to tell her, but she didn't understand.

The only person Indella would talk to was Marlys. All she would say were two words. "I tried." Over and over, those same two words. "I tried. I tried."

When they finally allowed her to come home, I was starting the fifth grade.

CHAPTER NINE
In The Shelter Of The Fold

1

This wasn't what you had bargained for. They turned the Cattle Squad into a regular military unit. It was their way of securing their secrets is your explanation. The Navy had been enough for you, and now you are in the Marines. Your hell continues to be bottomless. And you're not even dead yet.

You're awakened at five every morning for drills. You march for hours in the hot Nevada sun, going nowhere, doing nothing except moving your feet and lugging the fifty pounds of supplies strapped to your back. You recall thinking of yourself as a test rat. Recently, you've become a pack mule, a jackass, and an empty mass of human flesh built and trained to take orders from buffoons with half your intelligence.

You are tucked away in your bunk at nine each night. You're not allowed to talk, though, of course, you talk all the time to your buddies, all of who are ten years younger than you, none with families. They have no cares in the world. They wake up, follow orders, go to sleep. You envy them.

Your kids must be half grown by now. You wonder if Howbo is as sassy as ever or if Winston has outgrown his sissiness or if Trudy has become something other than everybody's dress-up doll. You wonder if Indella misses you. You wonder if she has found herself another man. You wonder if she's spending all the money you're sending her wisely or if at all. You wonder too much. It's easier to sleep than to remember. Sleep without dreams.

They keep telling your squad that they're priming you for the big blowout that's supposed to happen in the not too distant future. You ask your buddies if they know what they're talking about and of course they don't. These buddies are dumber than you, which isn't saying a whole hell of a lot. They hardly know how to shape an idea beyond basic needs. If an idea came into their heads, they'd drop over dead from the novelty of it.

So it's up to you to figure out all the ins and outs of what's planned for your future. You joined the Cattle Squad out of awe for the power of the sun. You've actually witnessed a few expressions of that power, once as close as twenty miles. That had been too close. You had felt the need to run, only you knew that your legs weren't strong enough to get you away. The light had been blinding, even though you were wearing the prescribed welder's goggles. The wind was what you remember most, though. The hurricane which came at you from across the desert was filled with sand and gravel and felt as if you were being hammered into unconsciousness. And that from an explosion twenty or more miles away. That was close enough to last you a lifetime.

Five a.m. and the command arrives: "Saddle up! Time to move it." So you do. You move it. Your pack is heavier than before. The standards are there: the goggles, the gas mask, the ear plugs, the protective vest, the steel cup for your family jewels, the leggings, the short handled spade, the steel helmet, and so on. This time there was food for an overnight and water for a week. You must be going on a joy trip, and you're not sure this is the fun your buddies seem to think it will be. You'd just as soon stay in your bunk and dream of home.

You're weary and wary of marching. The hell in which you find yourself isn't worth the hell in which you find yourself. You want out. You want home. You want your wife and kids. When you're back with them, you'll never leave them again. This you know for an absolute certainty. Your days of happy feet are finished. · The day of your service will soon be up, and you cannot wait. The longing that took you deep into this hell is nothing when compared to the longing you now have to return. If that is so, then why do you even now when you think of your wife and home and kids, you keep getting images of Omiya and Noriko in your head? Why is it that when you dream of sex, it is always with Omiya, not your wife? Are you sure your wandering is over? Will you ever be sure?

The trucks take you deep into the empty desert. You march from there in the early July sun with your life fluids dripping off your head and into the dust. No life here to take advantage of your sweat. Only emptiness. Only sand.

Your march takes you past a strange sort of prison. It contains maybe fifty men, all dressed the same: in tattered pants, no shirts, no shoes, no hats. They are inside a compound of barbed wire with only a single hut to provide them shelter. You call to them as you pass, but the few men standing at the wire don't seem to understand. It is as if your language is foreign to them. They stare with empty eyes. You think they might beg for food or water, but they don't seem to be either hungry or thirsty. Maybe your captain will let you take a break in the shelter of their hut, but you keep marching. You wonder: what have these men done to merit such treatment so far removed from the civilized world? Some horrid crimes, perhaps, crimes of an unforgivable nature. Crimes like deserting wife and children? Could they have been that bad?

You then take a breather at midday in the shade of a deserted village. There are eight buildings in all: one each made of wood, steel, tin, aluminum, bamboo, iron, stucco, and cement. Each building is the same: empty of life, empty of any sort of life-giving systems like electricity, running water, or sewage. You eat your lunch sitting at a table inside the bamboo house thinking that in a better world, such a house would be almost livable. Omiya could turn this hut into a home, one filled with beauty and grace.

Siesta time and you stretch out on a bed in the tin house. It is as soft as the cot back at the base, and the new shiny tin is effective in deflecting the heat of the sun so that it is almost pleasant. Not a bad way to spend a July afternoon.

"What day is it," you ask the captain who is stretched across the bunk next to yours.

"What does it matter? It's the third."

"Of July?" you ask.

"No, of fucking January. Will you leave me alone!"

The third of July. Tomorrow is your daddy's birthday. Which one will it be? How old? Is he still alive? Does it matter?

At about five you and your buddies are rousted up and ordered to empty the cardboard boxes that have been delivered to each of the houses. Easy enough of a task, so you think. The boxes are each the size of a man. Each contains a life-sized doll, mostly human, some animal. You are told to place the dolls, each dressed in pleasant colorful clothing, inside the houses. "Make them look lived in," you're told. "Place the dummies in or near windows or doors. We want to see them," the military bosses say. You follow their orders and put the dolls inside what are obviously play houses for the brass. They probably come here at night and do weird things to themselves.

"This is kinky," one of your buddies says. You've not heard that word before, "Kinky," so you don't know exactly how to respond except to nod and agree. If he thinks it's kinky, then he's probably right.

At seven and as the sun nears its daily disappearance, you are told to leave the strange little village and follow the captain up the ridge to the east. You obey. What else is there to do but obey? You march until there's no sun left and the cool desert breeze turns your sweat into ice. And still you march, hour after hour until you're ready to drop. You come to a low depression in the plain that looks as if it had been dug by a tractor with a plow. The captain tells you to start digging in, that you're to make sure you're deep enough in the earth to be able to not see out of your hole.

"This has turned creepy," you say to a buddy who is shoveling loose sand and gravel out of the trench.

"Creepy how?" he wants to know.

"Just creepy. Those lonely houses. That queer prison back there. Makes you wonder," you say.

"Wonder about what?"

And you can't answer him in a way he will understand. So you try another tact. "What if," you say, "all this is a test to see which kind of building can withstand a nuclear attack?"

"Makes sense," your buddy says.

"What if we're part of that test?"

"How do you mean?"

"What if they want to know if the Cattle Squad can withstand a direct hit from an enemy bomb?"

"We can."

"We don't know that."

"Sure we do. We're marines."

You almost laugh at his naive attitude. Yeah, marines are so tough they can withstand even an atomic bomb. Let the heavens rain hell for eighty days and eighty nights and the Marines will still be there, eager for the real action to begin. Aren't you glad you're holed up with such intelligent people? Doesn't it make you proud that this is what you left your wife and kids for? Aren't you ready to go back home yet?

The answer to that last question is. . .

"Batten it down," the captain says. "Get some rest. You'll be up early in the morning with a hell of a lot of work to do."

Only you can't rest. You write another letter to Indella in your head. You have so many letters inside you that you know they are running together, becoming entwined in such a way that you'll never be able to get them separated. Still, you don't have anything else to do with your brain. Might as well write imagined letters. "Dear wife, Your husband is a fool. He gave away the very things that bring meaning into his life, time with you, his kids, his family. He sacrificed all so he could come here and sleep in a sandy trench and where he will be asked to confront the ravages of hell come morning. They haven't told him yet if this is the case, but all the signals are there, everything is in place for him and all those as foolish as he to test their mettle against the most horrifying contraption on the face of the earth. He is still in awe of the power, the force, the gruesome nature of the beast. But he is missing you so dearly this night, the way you smell, the way you touch him, the way you ignite the essence of his soul. . ." "Dear Omiya," you begin again, "I hope you are well. . ."

You turn your brain off. It's that or start sobbing in the desert. You're a marine after all. Marines don't cry. They don't have tear ducts.

2

Family reunion that year was not a pleasant time for Indella. Hev and Marlys along with Martha and Beau, Brenda and her husband Drake, and Horatio's young wife, Leona, concocted the idea of bringing the family together the Fourth of July. That was the suspected birth of Alexander Stevens Cobb. What better reason to bring everyone together than to honor the family patriarch.

Alexander Stevens was getting older and May Lou was not doing as well as the family would have liked. So, the idea of a reunion to be held at the Douglasville City Park was solidified.

Indella and her three children were obliged to attend. Marlys had insisted on it. "You're the only vestiges of Howie Cobb left to us," she said, her prime argument.

"But Howie's not dead," Indella insisted. She was still getting the government checks the first of each month. If only he were, she had wanted to say.

Indella had met a young man from Atlanta who had been at Milledgeville the same time as she. Pedro Vera had suffered similarly to Indella, only he hadn't been so severe as to require the special operation. He had tried slashing his wrists with a sea shell during a vacation to Tybee Island. He didn't know why. He laughed about it and tried to assure everyone at the hospital that he was really quite well, that his so called suicide attempt was really a scientific experiment that had gotten a little out of hand. Regardless, he was in Milledgeville along with Indella. They spent a good deal of time together, time that was encouraged by the doctors as being healthy for both. Pedro was jovial, filled with jokes about himself and his life as a naturalized American citizen. He seemed to be attracted to Indella's quietness, to her pensive attitude toward life in general and toward her children in particular. He had been sent home a week earlier than she.

When she arrived at Glory Bea's following her six-month hospital stay, a bouquet of roses was waiting for her, signed to her mother's chagrin, "All my love, Pete." So, if Howie were dead, she could explore the options that Pedro Vera implied. This is what she wanted to say to Marlys but couldn't.

"Could I bring a friend?" Indella asked Marlys.

"Of course. The kids, too. Your Momma. Glory Bea would be most welcome."

"Oh, I don't think so. Momma Cobb and my Momma have never really gotten along."

"I'd forgotten about that." Marlys had heard about the roses, so she asked, "Is this a special friend? Someone I might know?"

"He's Spanish, lives in Atlanta."

"Oh, really?" Marlys became flirty momentarily. "I've never met a Spaniard before. You'll introduce me, won't you?"

"I doubt if he'll come."

"Insist!"

Howbo and Winston didn't care at all for Pete Vera when they met him. Trudy loved him immediately and even started calling him "Papa" with a little encouragement from Indella. Howbo was particularly unpleasant to the squatty little fellow with too much black hair and a tattoo on his left arm. The thing that Winston liked about him were his white teeth. When he smiled, which was quite a lot, his teeth sparkled like pearls. Pete owned his own automobile and even though his doctors had ordered him not to drive for at least the first six months back home, he was visiting the Howie Cobb family on a regular basis. Indella seemed to plan her days around Pete's arrivals. She primped for an hour each time she knew he was on his way. She even put lip-gloss on Trudy's face to make her prettier. Trudy was her favorite upon her return from the hospital. She put all her energy into making sure that her little girl was happy.

On the festive event of the first and soon to be annual Cobb family reunion, Pedro Vera provided escort for Indella and her children to the city park.

Pedro was welcomed by all. The women of the family were most interested in him and his background as an émigré from Barcelona before the war. He had fled Franco, he told them. They didn't know who Franco was, but that didn't seem to matter. They were intrigued by his tale of how he finally became a naturalized American citizen and how he had changed his name along with his new US identity. In Spain, he had been known as Pedro yParrar del Montez Vera Cruz. It was much simpler to be an American as Pete Vera. Sexy, too, according to Martha in one of her side remarks to Leona.

The meal was served under one of the open air pavilions at the park. It was only a short walk to the lake and its artificial beach and many of the youngsters spent their day in the water, splashing one another and soaking up the sun.

Pedro had never attended a family reunion. His family, as he told Horatio, Leona, and Beau, was still in Barcelona. To them, he was dead. Any time a Spaniard tosses aside his ancestral citizenship, he dies as far as the rest of his family is concerned. "It is our custom," he said.

Horatio asked him, "How's it feel being dead?"

Pedro responded by wiping his brow with a napkin and fanning himself against the July sun, "Hot."

To which Horatio said, "Well shoot, you might just as well be alive with the rest of us then!"

It was round two in the afternoon as a few of the older Cobbs were making ready to leave when Hank Cobb and his wife Frankie drove up in his fancy new Ford convertible. Everybody knew the automobile wasn't his. He had merely rented it for the day as a way to show off. The kids crowded around the car, wanting rides. "Later," Hank said, pushing the kids aside so he could hug the ladies.

Indella turned her back on Hank when he tried to give her a hug. "Good to see you looking so good," he said to her back.

"This is Hank Cobb?" Pedro Vera asked, his pearly teeth sparkling.

"You got that right, buddy," Hank said.

It occurred so fast, nobody was certain what actually happened. Some say Pedro took Hank down with a metal tray that had been used to hold fried chicken earlier. Others report that Pedro kneed Hank in the groin and then coldcocked him with Alexander Stevens' walking stick. Still others claim that Pedro clipped Hank on his jaw with a wicked right cross. Regardless of what happened, Hank was out cold before he hit the ground and had to be rushed to the hospital in his rented convertible Frankie, his wife, was convinced that her husband had a concussion and that if he did, she was going to sue.

"Sue me till tomorrow don't come," Pedro yelled into the convertible's dust. He added a few Spanish phrases, followed by a devilish laugh.

When the dust had settled, Pedro looked for Indella and the kids. But they were gone. Marlys and Hev had packed them into their car and taken them home.

That was the last Indella had to do with Pedro Vera. She never wanted to see him again. She announced to Marlys as she got out of the car at Glory Bea's that she was through once and for all with men.

3

Howbo came home from summer school with a new idea. It was one he had been studying in social studies, an idea that had never been expressed inside the Cobb household.

"Are you aware," Howbo said to his mother that evening during dinner, "that almost twenty five percent of American households are composed of a single parent?"

"Exactly what does that mean, son?" Indella asked.

"Well, that's what you are, Momma, a single parent."

"Is that a bad thing?" Trudy asked from her end of the table.

"Well, it's according," Howbo said, too full of a knowledge that needed some additional input. But he didn't know that. He was a parrot, come home with a new piece of information that in and of itself was at best a vapid reflection of the learning that he was actually doing in summer school, trying to remove some deficiencies. "Teacher says that single parent homes are endangering the American way of life."

"I don't understand what your teacher is trying to tell you," Indella said, enjoying a meal of her concoction, pound cake and pinto beans, a delicacy if there ever was one.

"She's saying that what we have in this house is un-American," Howbo said. He wasn't in agreement with his teacher, but there it was. As simple as he could make it.

"Don't we go to church?" Indella asked, waiting for an answer, one that only Howbo could provide.

"Yes, ma'am," he said, humbled.

"Ain't that American?" she persisted.

"Yes, ma'am."

"Then what's the problem?" she wanted to know.

"None that I can see," Howbo admitted. To silence Howbo at that point in time was an accomplishment, one that wasn't lost on Winston or Trudy, both sitting quietly, taking it all in. Howbo was at that point in his young life where if he found something new, it became the gospel and there was no way under the sun to dissuade him. But Indella had done it with a simple question, put Howbo and his "know it all" attitude in its proper place. It made Winston sad in a humble sort of way. He trusted Howbo's knowledge. He relied on him for the facts of life.

Surprisingly, Howbo wasn't finished. A little later, he ventured, "Our teacher says that divorce is changing the very foundation of the American social ethic."

"Really?" Indella said, serving everybody another slice of pound cake. This one she topped with a mixture of peaches, strawberries and cream. "Exactly what is this thing your teacher is calling 'divorce,' son?"

"I'm not sure. I think it has to do with the way you and Daddy are living, I mean, not together."

"Divorce is a little more complicated than that, Howbo. Your teacher should tell you that, too, if you ask me."

"So what is it then?"

Everybody was interested in this piece of information. "Divorce" was a word that kept coming up in conversations around Indella and her friends, especially when at church. It seemed to be a serious word since it was always said in a low tone of voice, close to a whisper. Winston assumed it was like cancer or smallpox or polio. Every time somebody had a case of one of these or similar diseases, the person who was doing the naming always resorted to a whisper. He thought perhaps it was an attempt to keep the gods, whoever they might be, from overhearing and causing the person who actually said the word "Cancer" or "Smallpox" or "Divorce" to develop the disease and die from it. So, when Howbo said the word a second time during dinner, both Trudy and Winston figured he was as good as dead in his tracks.

"Divorce," Indella said, "is a legal term. It's not a Christian thing to do. But a lot of people are doing it. It's when a man and a woman decide that they can no longer live together in a productive, family-type atmosphere. So, rather than cause a lot of anger, they decide to go to the courts and have their marriage ended. That ending is called a 'divorce.'"

"So what's a divorcee?" Winston asked. He had recently seen the film, *The Gay Divorcee* and found it confusing.

"That's a person, man or woman, who's gotten the courts to end their marriage."

"The Peabody's are divorced," Howbo said.

"That's right, they are."

"So what does that make Jeremy?" he wanted to know.

Indella had to think about that for a minute or two. Jeremy was probably the sweetest kid she knew, outside her own. She liked it when Howbo brought Jeremy Peabody home for supper. Jeremy always seemed to enjoy her food and was so polite about it. Finally, she said, "That makes Jeremy Jeremy. It doesn't change him in the least. In fact, his parents getting a divorce was probably the best thing to ever happen to Jeremy, if you ask me. It helped bring some definition to his life."

Howbo wasn't finished. There were more things that he wanted to know, and Winston could sense just where he was taking them. He tried to communicate to his brother not to go there, but Howbo wasn't paying any attention to him. He said, "So, are you and Daddy divorced?"

"No, we're not," she said without hesitation. The kids were so glad to hear her say that.

"Why not? You ain't lived together in over a year now."

"Because we haven't taken the matter to the courts, Howbo."

"Would you? I mean, since he's not here any more, could you take it to the courts, if you wanted to?"

"I guess so," Indella said. "Desertion is one of the reasons folks get divorced."

"Then, why don't you do it? Don't you think that Winnie, Trudy, and me need a little definition?"

Indella was quiet for a long time, giving serious thought to Howbo's serious question. Winston wanted to take a poke at his brother's teacher for putting such unnecessary thoughts into his head. The family was doing fine the way things were. He didn't need any definition, thank you very much. Indella was getting along with her occasional visits to the brain doctor she went to in Atlanta. Granny Bea didn't seem to mind that they were taking up room in her huge house. Trudy was getting ready to start to school and could already read better than Howbo. And Winston was learning loads of stuff, important stuff, stuff that didn't need to be discussed around the supper table.

But Indella must have considered Howbo's question worthy of her time. She put her fork down, steadied herself, and said, "Howbo, I have to admit. I've given some serious thought to the possibility of divorce, thinking that your father's desertion was cause enough for me to shake him off and get on with my life. In a way, it was my confusion over the divorce issue that caused me to spend those months away from you, my time in the hospital. I've sometimes thought that being a single parent was having a profoundly traumatic impact on the lives of you kids, that maybe you'd profit from have a daddy around the house, if for no other reason than to give you two boys a model to follow. I've even talked to your Aunt Marlys about this very same question."

"Really?" Winston said. If Indella discussed anything with Junior's mom, it must have been serious. Those two women, the kids noticed, loved each other too much to waste time talking about trivial things.

"Really," she said. "Whenever I give time to such a thought, I have to stop in my tracks and ask the question, 'Do I really hate your Daddy so much that I'd want to divorce him and turn all of you into poor orphaned tykes?' And the answer is always 'No.' I love him too much. Howbo, your Daddy may have deserted us, but I don't believe for an instant that he's ever stopped loving us. I am as convinced of that as I am of believing that God is good and will take care of us all, no matter what. Now. Does that answer your question?"

"Yes, ma'am," Howbo said. Winston didn't enjoy watching his older brother having to back down like that. It belittled him, and that wasn't the way things should be.

So Winston said, "Daddy will be coming home, soon."

Everybody at the table stopped eating. The legacy of his premonitions within the Cobb household was profound. All eyes turned to him. It was Trudy who broke the silence. "Really?" she said.

"Real soon," Winston said. He didn't know why he said that. He had no idea what he was talking about. As far as he knew, Howie Cobb was dead and buried on some remote South Pacific Island. But for some reason, he didn't back down. Everyone at the table seemed to need his premonitions. So he stuck to his guns. "He's pretty sick, sicker than he's ever been in his life," Winston said, "but he'll be home real soon."

The meal was finished in silence, each of the family lost in our own little worlds. Winston said a silent prayer that Howie Cobb wouldn't make a liar out of him and actually die on a deserted South Pacific island. That wouldn't have been fair.

4

The sun explodes the dark morning night. Only it isn't the same sun that God spun in his hands and set blazing in the heavens. It is the sun concocted by man in his clumsy fashion.

You had been shaken awake by the captain along with the rest of the test rats, told to dress for protection and then to stay low. Dress for protection. He means put the steel cup over your family jewels, plug your ears, hide your face with the gas mask and cover the eye holes with goggles. He means put the steel helmet on your head and stop using it as a piss pot or a pillow. He means, go deep in your hole, so deep they might cover you with dirt and call it quits.

"How close are we this time?" you ask the captain who is tinkering with his new toy, a Geiger Counter.

"Ten miles or so," he says.

Your brain refuses to comprehend what that means. "Ten miles. Jesus Christ, we might as well be at ground zero."

"Ten miles is ground zero, soldier. Now stop your complaining."

Your brain goes dead. It cannot process the concept of being where it is, doing what it is doing. It is so foolish, so stupid, so wasteful.

And you wait. The waiting is inevitable. It is what you do inside the Cattle Squad. It is what you practice most.

Waiting means thought. And that frightens you more. Thinking hurts you deep inside, down in the mystery of what makes you think in the first place. You've seen enough to know that there are some things that are best left to God, the inexplicable, the concept that knowledge equals results without regard to consequences. You sense it, in the deep place inside you, that God's creation is a circle, all points connected, woven together with threads of air and soil and water. Interrupt the weaving, and all hell breaks loose. This you know for an absolute certainty, that the brains-that-be, the children who play with atoms like tinker toys, are putting a chink in the circle, one that could lead to results no one can fathom. And for what? You are part of it, an infinitesimal part of creating the chink. What do you gain? It is no longer a matter of curiosity or whatever it was that drew you away from the circle God meant for you. Or are you wrong? Is family back home not your circle? Is your circle the one of Omiya and the cracked egg of her life?

You can't sleep, though sleep is the one thing you most want. A need to put an end to the constant contact with that deeper part of self. The idea of what God meant for you echoes inside you and will give you no rest. Such a thought, an instinctual notion that a greater being exists and that it, whatever it might be, is somehow aware of you and your idiotic smallness. You stare into the realm of the stars that on this night, without benefit of moon, are infinite in number. You let your brain go to them and creep with dismal understanding, trying to grasp the basic concept of "light year" or more fundamental than that, "eternity." You know you are not alone. You know that from the beginning of time, from that point where an eyelid first opened and permitted light, then recognition, then contemplation, that most living creatures have given at least a passing glance toward the heavens and felt like you feel right now, like mud, like part of a circle that should not--must not--be broken.

It is like shattered glass, the eruption that proves in an instant how true your feelings of being simplistic mud really are. The circle is gone, the connection to God severed, and nobody is smart enough to recognize the pieces.

First there is the light, more brilliant than a million suns. You see the insides of your hands, the bones and the large and small veins with blood being pumped through them. You see the inside of your skull and the pulsating brain tissue that for some reason has gone dull, feeling nothing, not even fear. Then the wind, being sucked into the vacuum of the light and you hug the earth with all your ant-like strength to keep from being sucked into the whirlwind of hell. The cloud of fire and dust and smoke and sand billows upward, it is as if you are part of it, being lifted free of the earth and its mortal constraints, being flung without resistance into the realm of God. Only this power, this force of the cosmos, is immoral and God will send you back, unwanted.

Then the blast arrives and you are flattened into the empty sand, being shoved whether you want to be or not into the bowels of the earth, sand becoming part of your skin, part of you, and you want to scream in defiance against the will of man that is trying to transform you, to remake your humanity. You want to rail against the loss of the earth's natural connectedness. Instead your scream is one of pain, severe, unrelenting pain. Only no one hears. No man. No God. All are screaming just like you, soundlessly, you, your buddies, God's circle. It is empty noise as the roar of the blast is such that it eats all other sound.

Now the heat. It is as if the air itself is in flames. The captain's hair is singed and so is yours. You recall that time in your other life when the fire storm in the Big Horns had nearly eaten you. There you had found the saving graces of water. It had protected you once, perhaps it will do so again. You souse yourself with the contents of your canteen, pouring the water over your face, now free of the searing mask, and letting it run under and over your shirt, bringing its near boiling heat in touch with your skin, and it soothes.

And finally another wind, this one blowing away from the rising cloud, taking with it sand and stone, hurling all in its path with a force equal to the breath of God, a force that only God has a need for. The captain's Geiger Counter has the sound of a popcorn popper and you know what that sound means. You are now one with Omiya, you have her illness inside you now and she can rest. She can slip into her grave with full knowledge that you can finally understand the trauma she had known, the pain she had suffered, the end of life as she had experienced it. You, like her, are now finished with the ultimate test. The circle with God is gone. The circle with Omiya is now complete. I know, I am aware. Omiya, I am you.

I stand with the rest of the Squad because the captain has ordered it. Move out, he says as he steps out of the protective trench. The sun, the real one this time, has brought the landscape into view. I can see the giant cloud, still growing upward with each pulsing second, a billowing monster of purple and red and brown, the colors of bruise and blood and grave. And I say to the captain as we begin our march toward the rising cloud, "What a way to spend the Fourth of July." He only nods. "Biggest fireworks display I've ever seen," I say.

The captain doesn't find the humor in my observation.

We reach the play village of eight houses. None remain standing. Only the one of steel has succeeded in retaining a semblance of its original shape. There are no dolls left for anyone to play with.

I realize I am a dead man when I find the cage. It, too, is of steel. I had not seen it before because it had been inside the concrete house, locked so no one could tamper with its contents. But now that the concrete is scattered like rubble, I see the cage and feel sickened by what it contains: the remains of what must have been a human torso, alive or dead at detonation makes no difference, the body still attached to the sides of the steel cage by a pair of handcuffs. The human being, if indeed what the cage contained had been human, had not gone willingly into the chink. It had been constrained, voided of any decision whether to or not to be part of man's test. I had been willing. I had chosen my path. The thing inside the cage: what choice had it had? What choices would it have made if given the chance? Are we any different, it and I, the thing in the cage that is totally burned and partially melted. What kind of world do we truly have, now that the tinker toys have been broken?

The captain, with his out-of-control Geiger Counter reminding us constantly of our irradiation, stands beside me and whispers, "What in God's name is that?"

"It's what it appears to be, sir. It's you and me, only we don't know it yet."

I let my pack drop to the crystallized sand. It sends a spray of what appears to be broken glass onto my military boots. I begin my stroll toward the rising sun, not knowing where I am going or caring one way or another. It is finally time that I begin my long journey home.

"Pick that pack up, soldier," the captain commands. I keep walking. "Pick it up now or I'll have you arrested."

I turn to him. He is such a little man, so insignificant. Like me. Like I've always been and always will be. At least I know who I am. "And then what, sir?" I ask him.

He can't answer me. I walk past the remainder of the make-believe buildings, past what must have been one of the plastic dolls, nothing remaining of it except half a hand with a finger pointing east, past what had been the special prison, the fencing mostly gone and only the rock foundation of the hut, empty now, no signs of life, no signs of any interest in life. I walk alone toward the sun, leaving a trail of military issue behind. When I reach the trucks and the pick-up point, I am naked and unashamed. And I am arrested for desertion of my post and kept in isolation so I cannot communicate these thoughts with anyone other than my own, miserable soul.

CHAPTER TEN
The Benefits Of A Life Poorly Lived

My prediction proved accurate. Howie came home sicker even than I had said he would be.

He died at the Veterans Hospital in Atlanta seven weeks after his return home. Cause of death on his death certificate was cancer of the lungs. The doctors told us that Howie Cobb had smoked himself to death. We didn't question it. We didn't know to.

He was thirty-six years old. I was eleven, almost twelve. I had hardly had time to get to know him.

Indella lived a widow's life, drawing checks from the government for services Howie had rendered that were never made known to us. She couldn't remarry. She would have lost the checks. So instead, she had a string of men through her small house down the hill from Granny Bea who would have challenged five women of equal abilities. It bothered Granny Bea who had to sit in her massive house, watching the cars come and go, knowing the sins her daughter was accumulating. When Indella was found by the mailman one morning hanging by the neck from the pecan tree out back, Granny Bea felt little remorse. At least with her suicide, if indeed that was what it was, the sinning came to an end.

Howell Junior runs a used car lot in Douglasville and Trudy married up, becoming the bride of the owner of a major trucking firm in Marietta. The firm had owned the truck that had smashed into the Pontiac so many years before, almost claiming Trudy's life at the age of three weeks. Life is full of these little ironies.

I went to college, studied marketing, and became a stockbroker, a life I have dearly despised. I invested wisely, taking a chance very early on a new emerging company devoted to cable television and it made me comfortable, and the envy of my older brother who wishes he had gotten in on the ground floor like I did.

It would be nice to say that Howie Cobb's story ended with his death in 1956. But that's not the way life is.

Just this past week, Howell, Trudy, and I each received a call from an estate lawyer from a major investment firm that I knew only by reputation as an organization to be greatly admired. Each of us was asked to meet him in his office on Peachtree Street in downtown Atlanta on a particular day at a particular time. The man made it sound imperative that we be there, the three of us together.

Howell called me on the phone first: "What is all this?" he wanted to know.

I had no idea. Neither did Trudy who called a little bit later. "See you at this man's office, I guess," was all I could say.

So we gathered. It was the first time the three of us had been together since Indella's funeral. We were uneasy with each other. Too many common memories, I suppose. We passed time while waiting in the estate lawyer's outer office, asking about each other and our separate lives. Trudy was pregnant with her third child; she hoped this one would finally be a girl; regardless this would be her last. At her age, she said, it was time to turn child bearing over to the young ones. Howell was dating a new woman, this one possibly being THE one for him. He had already gone through five failed marriages, the concept of divorce being one he endorsed without reservation. They didn't ask about Joseph, my lover. They didn't want to know. Homosexuality was something they both preferred to leave alone, afraid, I suppose, that if they articulated the word, they could possibly catch it.

Then Bartholomew Seville Banks came from his inner office and greeted us all as if we were long lost friends. "Just call me Bart," he said, to which Howell replied, "You can call me Mr. Cobb."

Bart led us into his inner office, a remarkable room of mahogany, steel, and glass, overlooking downtown Atlanta with a view of Stone Mountain in the distance. "May I get you anything? Something to drink?" he asked. We all declined. He smiled at Trudy and nodded. "So, when is the due date?" he asked.

"Six weeks, two days and fourteen hours," she said. She was ready for this, her final pregnancy, to be finished. "If he ain't ready by then, the doctors are taking the son of a gun. I'm sick and tired of his kicking me."

"So, it's a boy?"

"Bobby and me don't care to know. We like surprises," Trudy said.

"I suppose you're wondering why I've called you," Bart began, sitting back in his swivel chair that appeared to be real leather.

We all agreed that yes, we were curious and would be eager to find out the answer to his compelling question.

"My firm represents clients from around the world. One such client is a former member of the Japanese Diet, the honorable Akira Hashimoto, recently deceased, a victim of a heart attack in his Tokyo penthouse. Akira-san was quite a wealthy man, astonishingly wealthy in fact. He was the principal stockholder in several of the largest commercial enterprises in Japan as well as in Taiwan and Manila. You are a stockbroker, aren't you, Winston?"

"That's right," I said.

"Then you will understand what it would mean to be the recipient of one million shares of stock in Asiana Enterprises."

I gulped. I couldn't comprehend the figure. It was too large. "Who would be the recipient?"

"Why, you, your brother and sister. As the sole and only heirs of the long deceased Howell Madison Cobb, you are in line to receive what has been bequeathed to him by Akira-san."

The three of us sat stunned. We had no idea what he was talking about. Japan? Some dude in Tokyo croaks and leaves your father dead over forty years a mountain of money? "This makes absolutely no sense whatsoever," I said. Howell was too much in shock to take his accustomed role of leader of the family.

"You are not aware of the relationship between your father and Mr. Hashimoto?" the estate lawyer asked.

"No, we're not."

"Those of us in the firm were hoping you would be." He fiddled with a few papers on his desk. "We are talking about the right man here, Mr. Howell Madison Cobb of Douglasville, Georgia, son of Alexander Stevens and May Lou Cobb, both deceased, and husband of the late Indella Shealy Cobb, also of Douglasville."

"You've got the man all right," Howell said.

"It came as a surprise to all in our firm that Akira-san would name in his will, among sixty eight other Americans, your father. All those named had one thing in common: they had all served in some capacity aboard the USS Circe during the Second World War. In each case, Akira-san left one thousand shares of stock in one or more of his companies. However, to your father he left one million. Plus an additional puzzlement. He states in his will that your father is to be granted a pack of chewing gum, preferably Spearmint. He writes in his will that 'Spearmint saved my life by giving me hope for the future of mankind.'" The lawyer stared first at one of us, then at the other, looking obviously for some sort of recognition. But the three of us sat there dumbfounded, no clue as to what any of this meant.

"Since Mr. Cobb, his wife, and parents are all deceased, it is the decision of the probate courts in Tokyo and here in Atlanta that the bequeathment forthcoming from Akira Hashimoto go to you. Equally shared, of course. How would you like to receive your dispensation? Cash or bonds?"

Howell turned to me, a slight smile beginning to emerge on his face, "I guess that means we be rich, huh, Pooh?"

"But who the hell is this Hashimoto guy?" Trudy said, a question that nobody seemed able to answer.

Her question, a logical one and worthy, was not the question that needed an answer.